Also available

The Outer Limits, Volumes One and Two

with stories by

HARLAN ELLISON
DIANE DUANE
JOHN M. FORD
HOWARD V. HENDRIX
FREDRIC BROWN
MICHAEL MARANO
RICHARD A. LUPOFF

Edited by
Debbie Notkin

Prima Publishing

© 1997 Outer Productions Inc. All Rights Reserved.
The Outer Limits is a trademark of Metro-Goldwyn-Mayer Inc., and is licensed by MGM Consumer Products.

All rights reserved. No part of this book may be reproduced or transmitted in any form or by any means, electronic or mechanical, including photocopying, recording, or by any information storage or retrieval system, without written permission from Prima Publishing, except for the inclusion of quotations in a review.

"I, Robot" reprinted by permission of the author and the author's agent, Scott Meredith Literary Agency, L.P., 845 Third Avenue, New York, New York 10022.

PRIMA PUBLISHING and colophon are registered trademarks of Prima Communications, Inc.

ISBN: 0-7615-0621-7
Library of Congress Catalog Number: 96-67914
97 98 99 00 HH 10 9 8 7 6 5 4 3 2 1
Printed in the United States of America

How to Order:
Single copies may be ordered from Prima Publishing, P.O. Box 1260BK, Rocklin, CA 95677; telephone (916) 632-4400. Quantity discounts are also available. On your letterhead, include information concerning the intended use of the books and the number of books you wish to purchase.

Visit us online at http://www.primapublishing.com

*To the memory of my father,
who opened the books for me*

Contents

Foreword   ix
    David Schow

I, ROBOT   1
    Eando Binder

THE QUALITY OF MERCY   23
    Phoebe Reeves

THE VOYAGE HOME   97
    Diane Duane

THE FORMS OF THINGS UNKNOWN   167
    Richard A. Lupoff

Foreword

When the idea of anthologies comprised of novelized *Outer Limits* episodes was first proposed, it was met with overwhelming disinterest and incomprehension. I should know; it was 1979 and I was the one who proposed it to the head of what was then called United Artists Television Syndication.

Fortunately for you, just as the idea has now caught on, many of the contributors to this series have achieved their own stature on their own terms. Their abilities, it can be said, are now equal to the task of rendering these stories in prose, a task first suggested when they as writers were neophytes or unknown quantities . . . even though the stories that comprise this third volume in the series span nearly sixty years of storytelling.

"I, Robot" was first published in the January 1939 issue of *Amazing Stories* Magazine under the collaborative byline of "Eando" Binder—E-and-O standing for brothers Earl and Otto, though Otto Oscar Binder did most of the writing for this and the other Adam Link stories that were to follow. It is also the only story that links the old *Outer Limits* directly to the new, since the original episode, which co-starred a young Leonard Nimoy in a bit part, was remade for the Showtime revival of the series—now toplining Nimoy under the direction of his son, Adam. It should also be noted that Nimoy's parts in both shows, first as reporter Judson Ellis and later as DA Thomas Coyle, were not created by the Binders, but by scenarist Robert C. Dennis in 1964.

The embroidered Gothic melodrama of "The Forms of Things Unknown" is about as far away from the linear clockwork of "I, Robot" as can be imagined. Conceived by writer/producer Joseph Stefano as an elaborate evocation of the themes in both the classic Clouzot suspense film *Les Diaboliques* and Shakespeare (the title is part of a quotation found in *A Midsummer Night's Dream*), this closing episode of *The Outer Limits'* first season was written with two climaxes—one to serve the science fiction needs of the series, the other to provide a "rational" conclusion for an alternate version of the episode that was intended as a pilot for a proposed new show, *The Unknown,* to star Martin Landau as an investigator of the paranormal. The interpretation presented here by Richard A. Lupoff offers the latter story line with an intriguing fillip that expands the characters and offers a not-implausible grounding for their actions.

First to represent Showtime's *Outer Limits* is Brad Wright's "The Quality of Mercy"—another Shakespearean title (from *The Merchant of Venice*) used earlier on a 1961 episode of *The Twilight Zone*. This is apt because both stories are military table-turners, the snap in the tail of the latter-day story worthy of Rod Serling, rendered here courtesy of newcomer Phoebe Reeves.

After tackling the prose demands of another Stefano script in Volume One of this series, Diane Duane returns here with an adaptation of Grant Rosenberg's "The Voyage Home." Ms Duane's bailiwick in literature (thus far) is strongly slanted toward series tie-ins—from series of her own invention to tie-in books for TV and computer games. This makes her particularly nimble when it comes to novelizing a new show which is a revival of an old show; one must be up to the twists and turns.

There are certain dark, Gothic aspects of the original *Outer Limits* that gain an added dimension in prose form; I thought so in 1979 and I think so now. See for yourself if these narratives probe even deeper into the Inner Mind . . . or help you further past the outermost of limits.

David Schow
February 1997

Dr. Frankenstein's monster was made of flesh and blood; this creature describes himself as being made of "wheels and wires." The scientist/creator, Dr. Link, managed to infuse his creation not only with perception and movement, but with feelings and a moral code . . . but how can a robot so alien and terrifying get anyone to listen when he tries to explain how he feels—or what he meant to do?

I, Robot

by Eando Binder

My Creation

Much of what has occurred puzzles me. But I think I am beginning to understand now. You call me a monster, but you are wrong. Utterly wrong!

I will try to prove it to you, in writing. I hope I have time to finish—

I will begin at the beginning. I was born, or created, six months ago, on November 3 of last year. I am a true robot. I am made of wires and wheels, not flesh and blood.

My first recollection of consciousness was a feeling of being chained, and I was. For three days before that, I had been seeing and hearing, but all in a jumble. Now, I had the urge to arise and peer more closely at the strange, moving form that I had seen so many times before me, making sounds.

The moving form was Dr. Link, my creator. He was the only thing that moved, of all the objects within my sight. He and one other object—his dog Terry. Therefore these two objects held my interest more. I hadn't yet learned to associate movement with life.

But on this fourth day, I wanted to approach the two moving shapes and make noises at them. Particularly at the smaller one. His noises were challenging, stirring. They made me want to rise and quiet them. But I was chained. I was held down by them so that, in my blank state of mind, I wouldn't wander off and bring myself to an untimely end, or harm someone.

These things, of course, Dr. Link explained to me later, when I could dissociate my thoughts and understand. I was just like a baby for those three days—a human baby. I am not as other so-called robots were—mere automatized machines designed to obey certain commands or arranged stimuli.

No, I was equipped with a pseudo-brain that could receive *all* stimuli that human brains could. And with possibilities of eventually learning to rationalize for itself.

But for three days Dr. Link was very anxious about my brain. I was like a human baby and yet I was also like a sensitive, but unorganized, machine, subject to the whim of mechanical chance. My eyes turned when a bit of paper fluttered to the floor. But photoelectric cells had been made before capable of doing the same. My mechanical ears turned to best receive sounds from a certain direction, but any scientist could duplicate that trick with sonic-relays.

The question was—did my brain, to which the eyes and ears were connected, hold on to these various impressions for future use? Did I have, in short—*memory?*

Three days I was like a newborn baby. And Dr. Link was like a worried father, wondering if his child had been born a hopeless idiot. But on the fourth day, he feared I was a wild animal. I began to make rasping sounds with my vocal apparatus, in answer to the sharp little noises that the dog Terry made. I shook my swivel head at the same time, and strained against my bonds.

For a while, as Dr. Link told me, he was frightened of me. I seemed like nothing so much as an enraged jungle creature, ready to go berserk. He had more than half a mind to destroy me on the spot.

But one thing changed his mind and saved me.

The little animal, Terry, barking angrily, rushed forward suddenly. It probably wanted to bite me. Dr. Link tried to call it back, but too late. Finding my smooth metal legs adamant, the dog leaped with foolish bravery in my lap, to come at my throat. One of my hands grasped it by the middle, held it up. My metal fingers squeezed too hard and the dog gave out a pained squeal.

Instantaneously, my hand opened to let the creature escape! Instantaneously. My brain had interpreted the sound for what it was. A long chain of memory-association had worked. Three days before, when I had first been brought to life, Dr. Link had stepped on Terry's foot accidentally. The dog had squealed its pain. I had seen Dr. Link, at risk of losing his balance, instantly jerk up his foot. Terry had stopped squealing.

Terry squealed when my hand tightened. He would stop when I untightened. Memory-association. The thing psychologists call reflexive reaction. A sign of a living brain.

Dr. Link tells me he let out a cry of pure triumph. He knew at a stroke I had memory. He knew I was not a wanton monster. He knew I had a thinking organ, and a first-class one. Why? Because I had reacted *instantaneously*. You will realize what that means later.

———∽∽∽∽∽∽∽———

I learned to walk in three hours. Dr. Link was still taking somewhat of a chance, unbinding my chains. He had no assurance that I would not just blunder away like a witless machine. But he knew he had to teach me to walk before I could learn to talk. The same as he knew he must bring my brain to life fully connected to the appendages and pseudo-organs it was later to use.

If he had simply disconnected my legs and arms for those first three days, my awakening brain would never have been able to use them when connected later. Do you think, if you were suddenly endowed with a third arm, that you could ever use it? Why does it take a cured paralytic so long to regain the use of his natural limbs? Mental blind spots in the brain. Dr. Link had all those strange psychological twists figured out.

Walk first. Talk next. That is the tried-and-true rule used among humans since the dawn of their species. Human babies learn best and fastest that way. And I was a human baby in mind, if not body.

Dr. Link held his breath when I first essayed to rise. I did, slowly, swaying on my metal legs. Up in my head, I had a three-directional spirit-level electrically contacting my brain. It told me automatically what was horizontal, vertical, and oblique. My first tentative step, however, wasn't a success. My knee-joints flexed in reverse order. I clattered to my knees, which fortunately were knobbed with thick protective plates so that the more delicate swiveling mechanisms behind weren't harmed.

Dr. Link says I looked up at him like a startled child might. Then I promptly began walking along on my knees, finding this easy. Children would do this more except that it hurts them. I know no hurt.

After I roved up and down the aisles of his workshop for an hour, nicking up his furniture terribly, walking on my knees seemed completely natural. Dr. Link was in a quandary about how to get me up to my full height. He tried grasping my arm and pulling me up, but my three hundred pounds of weight were too much for him.

My own rapidly increasing curiosity solved the problem. Like a child discovering the thrill of added height with stilts, my next attempt to rise to my full height pleased me. I tried staying up. I finally mastered the technique of alternate use of limbs and shift of weight forward.

In a couple of hours Dr. Link was leading me up and down the gravel walk around his laboratory. On my legs, it was quite easy for him to pull me along and thus guide me. Little Terry gamboled along at our heels, barking joyfully. The dog had accepted me as a friend.

I was by this time quite docile to Dr. Link's guidance. My impressionable mind had quietly accepted him as a necessary rein and check. I did, he told me later, make tentative movements in odd directions off the path, motivated by vague stimuli, but his firm arm pulling me back served instantly to keep me in line. He paraded up and down with me as with an irresponsible oaf.

I would have kept on walking tirelessly for hours, but Dr. Link's burden of years quickly fatigued him and he led me inside. When he had safely gotten me seated in my metal chair, he clicked the switch on my chest that broke the electric current giving me life. And for the fourth time I knew that dreamless non-being which corresponded to my creator's periods of sleep.

My Education

In three days I learned to talk reasonably well.

I give Dr. Link as much credit as myself. In those three days he pointed out the names of all the objects in the laboratory and around. This fund of two hundred or so nouns he supplemented with as many verbs of action as he could demonstrate. Once heard and learned, a word never again was forgotten or obscured to me. Instantaneous comprehension. Photographic memory. Those things I had.

It is difficult to explain. Machinery is precise, unvarying. I am a machine. Electrons perform their tasks instantaneously. Electronics motivate my metallic brain.

Thus, with the intelligence of a child of five at the end of those three days, Dr. Link taught me to read. My photoelectric eyes instantly grasped the connection between speech and letter, as my mentor pointed them out. Thought-association filled in the gaps of understanding. I perceived without delay that the word "lion," for instance, pronounced in its peculiar way, represented a live animal crudely pictured in the book. I have never seen a lion. But I would know one the instant I did.

From primers and first-readers I graduated in less than a week to adult books. Dr. Link laid out an extensive reading course for me, in his large library. It included fiction as well as factual matter. Into my receptive, retentive brain began to be poured a fund of information and knowledge never before equalled in that short period of time.

There are other things to consider besides my "birth" and "education." First of all the housekeeper. She came in once a week to clean up the house for Dr. Link. He was a recluse, lived by himself, cooked for himself. Retired on an annuity from an invention years before.

The housekeeper had seen me in the process of construction in the past years, but only as an inanimate caricature of a human body. Dr. Link should have known better. When the first Saturday of my life came around, he forgot it was the day she came. He was absorbedly pointing out to me that "to run" meant to go faster than "to walk."

"Demonstrate," Dr. Link asked as I claimed understanding.

Obediently, I took a few slow steps before him. "Walking," I said. Then I retreated a ways and lumbered forward again, running for a few steps. The stone floor clattered under my metallic feet.

"Was—that—right?" I asked in my rather stentorian voice.

At that moment a terrified shriek sounded from the doorway. The housekeeper had come up just in time to see me perform.

She screamed, making more noise than even I. "It's the Devil himself! Run, Dr. Link—run! Police—Help—"

She fainted dead away. He revived her and talked soothingly to her, trying to explain what I was, but he had to get a new housekeeper. After this he contrived to remember when Saturday came and on that day kept me hidden in a storeroom reading books.

A trivial incident in itself, perhaps, but very significant, as you who will read this will agree.

Two months after my awakening to life, Dr. Link one day spoke to me in a fashion other than as teacher to pupil; spoke to me as man to—man.

"You are the result of twenty years of effort," he said, "and my success amazes even me. You are little short of being a human in mind. You are a monster, a creation, but you are basically human. You have no heredity. Your environment is molding you. You are the proof that mind is an electrical phenomenon, molded by environment. In human beings, their bodies—called heredity—are environment. But out of you I will make a mental wonder!"

His eyes seemed to burn with a strange fire, but this softened as he went on.

"I knew I had something unprecedented and vital twenty years ago when I perfected an iridium sponge sensitive to the impact of a single electron. It was the sensitivity of thought! Mental currents in the human brain are of this micro-magnitude. I had the means now of duplicating mind-currents in an artificial medium. From that day to this I worked on the problem.

"It was not long ago that I completed your 'brain'— an intricate complex of iridium-sponge cells. Before I brought it to life, I had your body built by skilled artisans. I wanted you to begin life equipped to live and move in it as close to the human way as possible. How eagerly I awaited your debut into the world!"

His eyes shone.

"You surpassed my expectations. You are not merely a thinking robot. A metal man. You are—life!

A new kind of life. You can be trained to think, to reason, to perform. In the future, your kind can be of inestimable aid to man and his civilization. You are the first of your kind."

The days and weeks slipped by. My mind matured and gathered knowledge steadily from Dr. Link's library. I was able, in time, to scan and absorb a page at a time of reading matter, as readily as human eyes scan lines. You know of the television principle—a pencil of light moving hundreds of times a second over the object to be transmitted. My eyes, triggered with speedy electrons, could do the same. What I read was absorbed—memorized—instantly. From then on it was part of my knowledge.

Scientific subjects particularly claimed my attention. There was always something indefinable about human things, something I could not quite grasp, but science digested easily, in my science-compounded brain. It was not long before I knew all about myself and why I "ticked," much more fully than most humans know why they live, think, and move.

Mechanical principles became starkly simple to me. I made suggestions for improvements in my own make-up that Dr. Link readily agreed upon correcting. We added little universals in my fingers, for example, that made them almost as supple as their human models.

Almost, I say. The human body is a marvelously perfected organic machine. No robot will ever equal it in sheer efficiency and adaptability. I realized my limitations.

Perhaps you will realize what I mean when I say that my eyes cannot see colors. Or rather, I see just one color, in the blue range. It would take an impossibly complex series of units, bigger than my whole body, to enable me to see all colors. Nature has packed all that in two globes the size of marbles, for *her* robots. She had a billion years to do it. Dr. Link only had twenty years.

But my brain, that was another matter. Equipped with only the two senses of one-color sight and limited sound, it was yet capable of garnishing a full experience. Smell and taste are gastronomic senses. I do not need them. Feeling is a device of Nature's to protect a fragile body. My body is not fragile.

Sight and sound are the only two cerebral senses. Einstein, colorblind, half-dead, and with deadened senses of taste, smell, and feeling, would still have been Einstein—mentally.

Sleep is only a word to me. When Dr. Link knew he could trust me to take care of myself, he dispensed with the nightly habit of "turning me off." While he slept, I spent the hours reading.

He taught me how to remove the depleted storage battery in the pelvic part of my metal frame when necessary and replace it with a fresh one. This had to be done every forty-eight hours. Electricity is my life and strength. It is my food. Without it I am so much metal junk.

But I have explained enough of myself. I suspect that ten thousand more pages of description would make no difference in your attitude, you who are even now—

An amusing thing happened one day, not long ago. Yes, I can be amused too. I cannot laugh, but my brain can appreciate the ridiculous. Dr. Link's perennial gardener came to the place, unannounced. Searching for the doctor to ask how he wanted the hedges cut, the man came upon us in the back, walking side by side for Dr. Link's daily light exercise.

The gardener's mouth began speaking and then ludicrously gaped open and stayed that way as he caught a full glimpse of me. But he did not faint in fright as the housekeeper had. He stood there, paralyzed.

"What's the matter, Charley?" queried Dr. Link sharply. He was so used to me that for the moment he had no idea why the gardener should be astonished.

"That—that thing!" gasped the man, finally.

"Oh. Well, it's a robot," said Dr. Link. "Haven't you ever heard of them? An intelligent robot. Speak to him, he'll answer."

After some urging, the gardener sheepishly turned to me. "H-how do you do, Mr. Robot," he stammered.

"How do you do, Mr. Charley," I returned promptly, seeing the amusement in Dr. Link's face. "Nice weather, isn't it?"

For a moment the man looked ready to shriek and run. But he squared his shoulders and curled his lip. "Trickery!" he scoffed. "That thing can't be intelligent. You've got a phonograph inside of it. How about the hedges?"

"I'm afraid," murmured Dr. Link with a chuckle, "that the robot is more intelligent than you, Charley!!" But he said it so the man didn't hear, and then directed him how to trim the hedges. Charley didn't do a good job. He seemed nervous all day.

My Fate

One day Dr. Link stared at me proudly.

"You have now," he said, "the intellectual capacity of a man of many years. Soon I'll announce you to the world. You shall take your place in our world, as an independent entity—as a citizen!"

"Yes, Dr. Link," I returned. "Whatever you say. You are my creator—my master."

"Don't think of it that way," he admonished. "In the same sense, you are my son. But a father is not a son's master after his maturity. You have gained that status." He frowned thoughtfully. "You must have a name! Adam! Adam Link!"

He faced me and put a hand on my shiny chromium shoulder. "Adam Link, what is your choice of future life?"

"I want to serve you, Dr. Link."

"But you will outlive me! And you may outlive several other masters!"

"I will serve any master who will have me," I said slowly. I had been thinking about this before. "I have been created by man. I will serve man."

Perhaps he was testing me. I don't know. But my answers obviously pleased him. "Now," he said, "I will have no fears in announcing you!"

The next day he was dead.

That was three days ago. I was in the storeroom, reading—it was the housekeeper's day. I heard the noise. I ran up the steps, into the laboratory. Dr. Link lay with skull crushed. A loose angle-iron of a transformer hung on an insulated platform on the wall had slipped and crashed down on his head while he sat there before his workbench. I raised his head, slumped over the bench, to better see the wound. Death had been instantaneous.

These are the facts. I returned the angle-iron back myself. The blood on my fingers resulted when I raised his head, not knowing for the moment that he was stark dead. In a sense, I was responsible for the accident, for in my early days of walking I had once blundered against the transformer shelf and nearly torn it loose. We should have repaired it.

But that I am his murderer, as you all believe, is not true.

The housekeeper had also heard the noise and came from the house to investigate. She took one look. She saw me bending over the doctor, his head torn and bloody—she fled, too frightened to make a sound.

It would be hard to describe my thoughts. The little dog Terry sniffed at the body, sensed the calamity, and went down on his belly, whimpering. He felt the loss of a master. So did I. I am not sure what your emotion of sorrow is. Perhaps I cannot feel that deeply. But I do know that the sunlight seemed suddenly faded to me.

My thoughts are rapid. I stood there only a minute, but in that time I made up my mind to leave. This again has been misinterpreted. You considered that an admission of guilt, the criminal escaping from the scene of his crime. In my case it was a full-fledged desire to go out into the world, find a place in it.

Dr. Link, and my life with him, was a closed book. No use now to stay and watch ceremonials. He had launched my life. He was gone. My place now must be somewhere out in the world I had never seen. No thought entered my mind of what you humans would decide about me. I thought all men were like Dr. Link.

First of all I took a fresh battery, replacing my half-depleted one. I would need another in forty-eight hours, but I was sure this would be taken care of by anyone to whom I made the request.

I left. Terry followed me. He has been with me all the time. I have heard a dog is a man's best friend. Even a metal man's.

My conceptions of geography soon proved hazy at best. I had pictured earth as teeming with humans and cities, with not much space between. I had estimated that the city Dr. Link spoke of must be just over the hill from his secluded country home. Yet the woods I traversed seemed endless.

It was not till hours later that I met the little girl. She had been dangling her bare legs into a brook, sitting on a flat rock. I approached to ask where the city was. She turned when I was still thirty feet away. My internal mechanisms do not run silently. They make a steady noise that Dr. Link always described as a handful of coins jingling together.

The little girl's face contorted as soon as she saw me. I must be a fearsome sight indeed in your eyes. Screaming her fear, she blindly jumped up, lost her balance, and fell into the stream.

I knew what drowning was. I knew I must save her. I knelt at the rock's edge and reached down for her. I managed to grasp one of her arms and pull her up. I could feel the bones of her thin little wrist crack. I had forgotten my strength.

I had to grasp her little leg with my other hand, to pull her up. The livid marks showed on her white flesh when I laid her on the grass. I can guess now what interpretation was put on all this. A terrible, raving monster, I had tried to drown her and break her little body in wanton savagery!

You others of her picnic party appeared then, in answer to her cries. You women screamed and fainted. You men snarled and threw rocks at me. But what strange bravery imbued the woman, probably the child's mother, who ran up under my very feet to snatch up her loved one? I admired her. The rest of you I despised for not listening to my attempts to explain. You drowned out my voice with your screams and shouts.

"Dr. Link's robot!—it's escaped and gone crazy!—he shouldn't have made that monster!—get the police!—nearly killed poor Frances!—"

With these garbled shouts to one another, you withdrew. You didn't notice that Terry was barking angrily—at you. Can you fool a dog? We went on.

Now my thoughts really became puzzled. Here at last was something I could not rationalize. This was so different from the world I had learned about in books. What subtle things lay behind the printed words that I had read? What had happened to the sane and orderly world my mind had conjured for itself?

Night came. I had to stop and stay still in the dark. I leaned against a tree motionlessly. For a while I heard little Terry snooping around in the brush for something to eat. I heard him gnawing something. Then later he curled up at my feet and slept. The hours passed slowly. My thoughts would not come to a conclusion about the recent occurrence. Monster! Why had they believed that?

Once, in the still distance, I heard a murmur as of a crowd of people. I saw some lights. They had significance the next day. At dawn I nudged Terry with my toe and we walked on. The same murmur arose, approached. Then I saw you, a crowd of you, men with clubs, scythes and guns. You spied me and a shout went up. You hung together as you advanced.

Then something struck my frontal plate with a sharp clang. One of you had shot.

"Stop! Wait!" I shouted, knowing I must talk to you, find out why I was being hunted like a wild beast. I had taken a step forward, hand upraised. But you would not listen. More shots rang out, denting my metal body. I turned and ran. A bullet in a vital spot would ruin me, as much as a human.

You came after me like a pack of hounds, but I outdistanced you, powered by steel muscles. Terry fell behind, lost. Then, as afternoon came, I realized I must get a newly charged battery. Already my limbs were moving sluggishly. In a few more hours, without a new source of current within me, I would fall on the spot and—die.

And I did not want to die!

I knew I must find a road to the city. I finally came upon a winding dirt road and followed it in hope. When I saw a car parked at the side of the road ahead of me, I knew I was saved, for Dr. Link's car had the same sort of battery I used. There was no one around the car. Much as a starving man would take the first meal available, I raised the floorboards and in a short while had substituted batteries.

New strength coursed through my body. I straightened up just as two people came arm-in-arm from among the trees, a young man and woman. They caught sight of me. Incredulous shock came into their faces. The girl shrank into the boy's arms.

"Do not be alarmed," I said. "I will not harm you. I—"

There was no use going on, I saw that. The boy fainted dead away in the girl's arms and she began dragging him away, wailing hysterically.

I left. My thoughts from then on can best be described as brooding. I did not want to go to the city now. I began to realize I was an outcast in human eyes, from first sight on.

Just as night fell and I stopped, I heard a most welcome sound. Terry's barking! He came up joyfully, wagging his stump of tail. I reached down to scratch his ears. All these hours he had faithfully searched for me. He had probably tracked me by a scent of oil. What can cause such blind devotion—and to a metal man!

Is it because, as Dr. Link once stated, that the body, human or otherwise, is only part of the environment of the mind? And that Terry recognized in me as much of a mind as in humans, despite my alien body? If that is so, it is you who are passing judgment on me as a monster who are in the wrong. And I am convinced it is so!

I hear you now—shouting outside—*beware that you do not drive me to be the monster you call me!* . . .

The next dawn precipitated you upon me again. Bullets flew. One struck the joint of my right knee, so that my leg twisted as I ran. One smashed into the right side of my head and shattered the tympanum there, making me deaf on that side.

But the bullet that hurt most was the one that killed Terry!

The shooter of that bullet was twenty yards away. I could have run to him, broken his every bone with my hard, powerful hands. Have you stopped to wonder why I didn't take revenge? Perhaps I should! . . .

I was hopelessly lost all that day. I went in circles through the endless woods. I was trying to get away from the vicinity, from your vengeance. Toward dusk I saw something familiar—Dr. Link's laboratory.

My birthplace! My six months of life here whirled through my mind with kaleidoscopic rapidity. I wonder if my emotion was akin to what yours can be! Life may be all in the mind. Something gripped me there, throbbingly. The shadows made by a dim gas-jet I lit seemed to dance around me like little Terry had danced. Then I found the book *Frankenstein* lying on the desk whose drawers had been emptied. Dr. Link's private desk. He had kept the book from me. Why? I read it now, in a half hour, by my page-at-a-time scanning. And then I understood!

But it is the most stupid premise ever made: that a created man must turn against his creator, against humanity, lacking a soul. The book is all wrong.

Or is it? . . .

As I finish writing this, here among blasted memories, with the spirit of Terry in the shadows, I wonder if I shouldn't . . .

It is close to dawn now. You have me surrounded, cut off. In the light you will rout me out. Your hatred is aroused. It will be sated only by my—death.

I have not been so badly damaged that I cannot still summon strength and power enough to ram through your lines and escape. But it would only be at the cost of several of your lives. And that is the reason I have my hand on the switch that can blink out my life with one twist.

Ironic, isn't it, I have the very feelings you are so sure I lack?

(signed) Adam Link

"EANDO" BINDER *was the rather unwieldy pseudonym of two brothers, Earl and Otto Binder, who combined their first initials with the word "and" to form the name under which they wrote science fiction. While their name may have been unwieldy, their stories were not. Adam Link, the protagonist of this tale, first appeared in this story in 1938. He soon became a mainstay of* Amazing Stories, *one of the leading science fiction magazines of the time. Together and separately, both brothers wrote for the comics (including doing ten years of continuity for* Captain Marvel), *as well as writing and editing science fiction, from the 1930s through the 1960s. Their work with Adam Link was a major influence on Isaac Asimov's robots, which have in turn affected all other science fiction about robots for the last fifty years.*

"The quality of mercy is not strained," says Portia in Shakespeare's The Merchant of Venice. *But the situation John Skokes finds himself in is more than strained. Being captured by the aliens is perhaps his greatest fear. Finding a human woman in the cell with him, a woman he is honor-bound to protect and save, is worse than his wildest imaginings. And what the aliens are doing to her is worse yet.*

The Quality of Mercy

Adaptation by Phoebe Reeves
Original Screenplay by Brad Wright

He tried to remember how the handful of fighter pilots who'd made it back had described Them, but his mind jammed on two images: a grade school textbook picture of a gray-brown, twenty-foot-long crocodile crawling onto a cracked river bank, and the shiny, knife-edged, obsidian rock face of the canyon wall near the family home where his white father had beaten him until he almost died. *Eight,* Major John Osceola Skokes kept thinking, lying on his side—*eight what? Feet high? Feet long? Number of them?* But the constant metallic clink of rocks hitting together underwater kept breaking up his thoughts.

He'd known They knew of him, about him. Skokes's name and fierce bravery as one of the last great

Seminole warriors had spread deep into space, across the vast expanse of the alien war—so quickly, in fact, that the Es-ta-had-kee, the white leaders of Earth's central fighter council (which included his father), were finally forced to acknowledge the Indian legacy, pride, and power that lay beneath his blond hair and blue eyes. And yet, it hurt him deeply that the public recognition of his heritage, which had brought him so much joy and so much pain, came from the exhausting hate of an impersonal, senseless war.

"I will not surrender to this meaninglessness," he had said quietly to himself as he boarded his ship amid the polite applause of the council and his fellow fighter pilots. For his first act as the leader of the last hidden defense squadron around the heart of Earth, the E-pof-caw, Skokes had war-painted his spacecraft so They'd prey on him. "I know the swamp, I am the swamp!" he'd war-whooped, waving and thrusting his Seminole mother's hunting knife at the two rippling black shapes that kept swallowing the stars in front of him as his ship danced Them far away from the location of his father and the rest of the hidden fleet. Somehow, though, he missed the third, star-glutted black maw that floated up behind him.

He lost his knife the moment the craft hit the ground. On impact, It yanked him over the twisted steel points of the ruined ship, dragging his lacerated limbs through pools of rocket fuel. His bruised body shivered uncontrollably, pulled along by the same indifferent force that had dragged his ship out of the air. The sound of rocks hitting underwater increased in tempo. His head ached with cold. They or It had blotted out the infinite night sky, and it was only by looking backwards and upside down as his head bumped along the rocky ground that Skokes saw the laser points of the ancient, familiar stars wink out. Willing himself not to lose consciousness, he bit through part of his tongue rather than allow the scream that choked him to explode.

A warrior never screams, his father had drilled into him.

A darker blackness choked off his last breath of vast, cold sky. Ragged, sharp, dripping, it pulsed and throbbed, searing the breath in his chest, even as it crushed his bones down onto the boiling air in his lungs. Not caring that the scalding damp had turned his flesh water soft, Skokes lashed out against the squeezing, dripping tunnel walls, while the Thing kept dragging him along, indifferent to how the jagged rocks sliced into his flesh like jellyfish.

When It finally stopped, Skokes bucked, renewing his kicks and punches, but It ignored him. The sound of rocks hitting together underwater increased in pitch and frequency, and a piece of the wall scraped away to reveal a cramped, roughly triangular interior area. It flicked him inside. Immediately, the pressure lessened. Despite the room's hot, sodden air, the cessation of the hideous pressure gave Skokes the relief burst he needed. Immediately he flung himself at the closing door. A blast of steam scalded his sliced skin just as he grabbed the edge of the door, and the toothy rock chomped off the skin of his fingertips.

Skokes doubled over, pressing his bloody fingers into his armpits. Determined to keep himself from passing out, he let out the tribal battle cry his father had taught him from his mother. "Yo-ho-e-hee!" The cell's heat and damp pushed on him again. "Yo-ho-e-hee! Yo-ho-e-hee!" The three banshee wails ripped into each other and hurtled off the walls, piercing even Skokes's hearing. One of the Es-ta-had-kee, the white fighters in his squadron, once described it as the sound of a holiday in Hell. For some reason though, the cry of rage didn't comfort him this time, and he began to hyperventilate. *They could have killed me, but They didn't. Why?* His mind returned to the last battle strategy meeting several days before. "Soldiers must often abandon those verities they defend: peace, human kindness, love. For they hold no meaning to our Enemy, and It will not bow to their supremacy. To win, we must become what we despise and despise what we become," Skokes had warned his troops the evening before they left on this mission. His father's grim gaze had burned into his head as he spoke, despite the fact that Skokes couldn't see him sitting in the shadows at the back of the room. "In the dark hours of the great battle ahead, you—we—cannot forget who and what we are." He'd had to keep pausing to slow his breathing, to calm the horrifying thrill racing his heart. How long had it been since any of them had seen Earth? They'd set up a defense light years from Earth that was barely close enough to guard the planet, and yet barely far enough to keep Them at bay. He'd shouted out the next words. "Earth's E-pof-caw squadron—we're the area around the heart! And so we must protect the heart! We are all that remains!" *The Aliens obviously don't know I don't have any issues with death,* he thought proudly, remembering his words to the fighters.

His head ached as he limped around the room, his feet sinking where portions of the rock floor turned flesh-soft. Some kind of organic bulb or polyp projected downward, casting a pale blue glow which alternately brightened and dimmed at sporadic intervals. Two unevenly-shaped holes, one filled with what appeared to be clear water and detritus, and the other with what looked like poisonous, brackish water rimmed with large salt-like crystals, took up most of the center of the cave cell. Where the uneven ground turned rock hard, the damp air had condensed to make it extremely slippery. Around the perimeter ran a ledge, roughly three feet high, and three feet deep. Skokes leapt towards the ledge and slid, landing on his hands and knees in slime. Struggling to his feet, he heard the tinny clinking of stones underwater and turned to the right where the wall door was.

To his left, something pale slid off the shelf. For a hideous moment, he thought he saw a pile of obsidian rocks fall to the ground and he freaked as a skeleton sat up on the shelf. "Yo He Wah," he gasped, "No. Mother." Then the form leaned out of the shadows into the dim light. It wasn't his mother's skeleton, but a person in a flight uniform. *They're trying to frighten me. Well, I'm not going to let Them.* He chided himself silently for letting his own shock get to him. Nothing They could have planned in this.

The person's face stayed in shadow as her body leaned forward. The woman slumped against the wall, her skin paler than could be blamed even on the polyp's dim glow. Her cropped hair stood up every which way and her face, despite its gaunt, high cheekbones, was so young she could have been fourteen. Though she was lean, Skokes could clearly see the soft, heavy curve of her breasts through the body layer of her torn, filthy clothing. Her eyes gleamed in the shadows.

He stayed where he was and drew himself up. "Who're you?"

Cocking her head from one side to the other, she coughed and rasped almost as though she'd forgotten how to speak. She opened her mouth and a guttural, bubbling croak came out. Skokes stumbled backwards and fell, but the woman made another sound, this time a groan, and he realized what he'd originally heard must have been her first attempt at language in who knew how long. At the same time, Skokes heard the stones hitting underwater again. He tensed and the woman tensed with him. They looked towards the prison door.

"Tristan," she whispered finally, after the clinking stopped. She cleared her throat. "Bree Tristan." She came out of the shadows. Her uniform was that of an Exeter fighter.

Tristan. Tumult, din. But she doesn't look like she's war whooped in her life. "You're a fighter?" he asked, a little too loudly.

She nodded, her head down.

He shook his head. "That's not possible. You're a woman. You can't be fighting in this war. They wouldn't have let you. I wouldn't have let you." He knew how it sounded, but women fighting would have meant the end of Earth, the end of life. The legend and legacy of his mother's people was that women were the ones who fought the Original War against the formlessness of the darkness of the universe before life. They were the great warriors of creation; they had given their lives to create others' lives. The sacred duty of the male warriors was to fight always to return the favor of their lives, to defend the greatest warriors. "Your mother was one of the greatest warriors, you'll always be giving your life for what she gave you," his father had told him as he had kicked and punched his son to near death next to the obsidian rock pile of his mother's grave.

The woman in the flight suit didn't say anything. Skokes swallowed, his heart thudding in his ears like doors slamming far away. *Women wouldn't have been given up—they couldn't have been. How long have I been out that so much would have changed?* "Rank and unit?" The question calmed him, and he took a deep breath of hot, humid air.

Bree winced as she straightened to stand at attention. "Sir . . ." she said, raising her hand to her brow.

"Cadet, second class . . . Europa base." She took a step forward, her eyes still in shadow. Again he heard the clicking of stones underwater, again they both looked in the direction of the cell door.

In that same second, she stumbled and slid, hitting her knee on a rock. He helped her up, but recoiled and grimaced at the sharp, metallic smell of blood and something else that stung his nose.

"Europa's in the defense perimeter," he said impatiently.

"Yes, it is." She nodded vigorously.

He snorted, as much to cover the exquisite pain of the slices in his rot-soft exposed skin as at her bloody body smell. "You're telling me you're a fighter pilot. You flew an Exeter fighter."

She paused before speaking. "Only a trainer." She coughed. "I got captured before I ever saw the inside of an Exeter."

He stopped, stunned, feeling a mix of superiority and horror. "How long have you been here?"

Gingerly, she picked her way back to the bench. Grabbing a handful of filthy rags, she mopped between her legs. Her flight suit was stripped down to the body layer and ragged black stains ran down the once white legs. The blood smell stank of bitter metal and spoiled meat and saturated the air. Skokes jerked his head back, blinking as he instinctively put his wrist to his nose. "It's hard to tell. But if my cycle is still every twenty-eight days like it was on Earth—just over three months."

Skokes shivered. *That's our clock?* He looked around the cell. A dried hairy algae-like substance stuck out in spikes along the entrance to the cell, clearly burned dead by the steam heat from Their weapons. Further into the room, moist lichen-type vegetation grew like cilia along the cracks and crevasses of the rocky floor. Skokes felt around the walls, wincing as the moisture saturated the slices in his hands. "The second Europa raid," he said, trying to keep his voice neutral.

"I was with my commander in a two-man trainer...." She cleared her throat and spoke faster. "We were practicing a refueling scoop in the Jovian atmosphere when we were hit pulling five G's while climbing out. I thought I'd just made some kind of mistake, that I'd lost control ... I remember screaming ... spinning.... They just seemed to pull us out of the sky like we were nothing."

Skokes's hands momentarily stopped their search. *Like being snapped out of the air by that indifferent, swaying force.* He nodded, even though he knew she couldn't see him in the dark corner of the cell.

Bree continued. "I remember the commander shouting something, the ejection system firing...."

"So he did try to protect you?"

She nodded. "I woke up here...." There was a catch in her voice.

He bit his tongue. *She was afraid. How could the greatest warriors be afraid?* "Alone?" He could hardly bear to face her, ashamed to find himself thinking what his father would have killed him for.

"No." Her voice got lower. "With the commander."

"What was his name?" Skokes continued. He had to keep his mind on the right protocol, the right order.

"Hartley."

Skokes frowned. "I don't know him." He turned to look at her and waited a moment, choosing his words carefully. "And I know everyone in this war."

Bree raised a hand to her face and rubbed her eyes, revealing what appeared to be an ugly bruise or burn along her forearm. It looked black in the dim light.

"What's that?" Skokes said sharply, upset.

Bree immediately pulled her arm in and shielded it against her belly.

"Show me your arm," he demanded.

Bree stepped back and Skokes heard the clicking of stones underwater. She glanced so quickly towards the door she stumbled again. Hurrying to her side, he grabbed her arm and jerked her to her feet.

Pulling her over to where the light was brightest, he examined the dark patch on her forearm.

Brownish-black triangular knobs jutted out of the skin. In the furrows between the rough, raised scales, purplish-blue placental skin bubbled like tiny man-o-war jellyfish. Engorged red and blue veins snaked out of the patch, rooting into the surrounding pale skin even as Skokes watched.

Bile burned the back of his throat, and he dropped her arm.

Bree kept her face lowered, but even in the poor light he could see her cheeks flush. "What is it?" Skokes asked quietly.

"A skin graft... Their skin."

"Why?" he whispered, more to himself than to her.

"I think They're trying to change me," she stopped, racked by coughing, "into one of Them."

For the first time, Skokes could see her eyes. Pale gray? green? He couldn't tell in the bluish light. He peered into her face. They looked almost... yellow, flecked with dark—black?—chips. Her pupils slid open in the dim light, swallowing up the pale irises. He drew back, remembering the stars gulped down by the rippling dark shapes. *Women are the greatest warriors, they were the creators. We owe them our lives—to let them die is the greatest shame,*" his father's voice sounded in his ears. Skokes flinched, feeling the boot in his ribs again.

"I make you sick," she said quietly, "I wish I'd died with Hartley."

Skokes glanced around the room. *I have to get us out of there. I need my hunting knife to cut that... thing off her, out of her.* "Sa-lof-ka-fots-kee! My hunting knife—how could I have lost it? I've been in crashes before and not let go of it!" He berated himself, unable to forget seeing the swollen blue vein slither below the surface of her skin and disappear. He glanced up at the living light, which had begun a cycle of glowing more brightly. *Tristan's a soldier— she'll know that I have to do what I'm about to do to her.*

I'll burn it off. And she'll bear the pain. If she is a soldier. He reached up. The bulb cringed, dimming as it pulled away from his groping fingers.

"If you touch them," Bree said, sighing, "they stop giving off light for hours."

He nodded, staring at it a moment longer before moving to the walls, scanning them for any kind of weapon. *She's taken stock of her surroundings at least.* "Can They hear us?" he said, keeping his voice low. He put an ear to the wall, feeling it carefully the whole time. "Are They listening?" He gave no impression he was paying any attention to Bree.

He felt her moving up behind him. He whirled around. She still sat in the same spot where she'd been. "I don't know," she answered, eyes fixed on the floor.

Skokes continued to survey the ragged walls, pushing at every surface, carefully poking his bleeding fingertips into any cracks and crevasses he came across. "Have They done anything that made you think They were?" He looked over his shoulder at her.

Bree shook her head. "No."

He took a deep breath and faced her. "Good. What else can you tell me?" *We are soldiers, not cowards.* He drew himself up and assumed a formal stance. "D'you know what rock we're on?"

Bree stood taller, too. "You never told me your name . . . sir."

He nodded and half smiled in spite of himself. *So you* are *a warrior.* "Skokes. Major John Osceola Skokes. Alpha wing."

She nodded wearily, sat down, and crossed her arms on her knees. "The commander spent hours doing what you're doing. . . ." She dropped her head down on her arms.

He clenched his jaw. "Es-ta-had-kee. White Man." He drew himself up proudly. "The commander didn't have Seminole blood in him."

She lifted her head immediately. "I didn't know, with your blond hair and blue eyes."

He frowned and blushed at the too-familiar offense, and wondered that she didn't seem to know who he was. But beneath these more frequent feelings, he found himself strangely flattered and disturbed that she'd been looking at him so closely. For the first time, he felt thankful for the dim light. "How can you see in this light?"

Her head cocked oddly to one side again. "I guess I'm just used to it. By now." Her lip quivered. "I'm sorry, sir—Major. It's just that. . . ."

"Was he here with you?" Skokes asked more gently.

"Until he died." She swallowed and took a moment to continue. "Until long *after* he died. They just . . . left him, as if I was supposed to do something with the body. . . ."

Why is she looking at me? For understanding? Skokes frowned at her, shocked. "You did make a mound for him, didn't you?"

She came back at him quickly. "Please sir, I didn't mean . . . I touched him once—to close his eyes—because he kept staring at me. Then I tried to cover him with the shells of the creatures they give us for food. I started with his head because of the eyes. It took so long because after he died, They only brought one creature at a time. I had half of him covered when They took him away."

Skokes didn't know what to say. "Even my Es-ta-had-kee, my white man father, beat it into me that the bodies of our fallen fellow warriors are to be protected at all cost." *Hartley's body has been carried off. But here They are taking Tristan's body while she lives.* He slammed his fist against the wall in frustration, trying to push away the hideous pictures of what they'd done with Hartley's body, the ravenous parasitic veins in Bree's arm. *The damn things probably eat Their dead.* "Hartley didn't find *anything?*"

Bree went back to her ledge. As soon as she sat down, she slumped forward, her head in her hands. "He couldn't move around very well. He lost part of his legs early on in the war—that's why he was an instructor."

Skokes gritted his teeth and nodded.

Bree continued. "He said we couldn't be on the Alien homeworld because they've calculated it at over two gravities. . . . He decided this moon or asteroid or whatever it is was just under one G."

"That's about right," Skokes said, nodding, relieved, "That's good."

"Is it?" Bree raised her head. At first her eyes were dark caverns on her thin, pale face, but as they caught the light, they shone like two balls of blue fire through the murky dimness.

"It means we've got a shot at getting out of here...." Skokes moved towards her, motioning with his open hand toward the wall containing the original door. "Getting off Their homeworld would have been—"

"There is no way out, Major." Her voice was controlled, but angry. "How? They're a hundred times stronger than we are. The walls are made of a crystal that's as hard as diamond—harder probably—"

"There's a way—"

"They'll torture you like the commander—"

"And I've never been tortured? I know what it's like to be at the brink of Il-it, at the brink of death." He stood right in front of her now. "Listen to me—"

"I can't watch that again—"

Now Skokes was angry. "Listen to me, *Cadet*. I intend to get out of here and back into the fight because *I have to*."

"*He* said the same thing—"

"He was a cripple—I'm *not*." He shook her and recoiled as the alien patch on her arm twisted under his grip. But he made himself hold on. *I have to protect us. I am the leader of E-pof-caw, the group around the heart which is Earth, and this woman is one of the greatest warriors. But why does she seem to slash open my own e-fee-caw—my own heart?* Skokes's protective feelings toward her couldn't staunch the blood-flow of private pain as the sudden, ferocious ache in his heart heaved the words out of him. "My father beat me so badly he almost killed me. My mother died in childbirth, but my father waited until I turned thirteen before he turned his rage on me for my betrayal of the greatest warriors. It would have been easy to die, but I didn't. I lived." He turned away and began examining the cell again, unconsciously wiping his hands harder than he needed to against the wall, trying to wipe away the feel of the rough reptilian skin.

Bree lashed out. "You think it's just a one-time clubbing where They crunch your bones in their teeth until you scream and then throw you back in? They took him away every day, and every day They brought him back a little less alive. . . ."

Skokes whirled around, furious. "Do you think I'd break under that? Do you think I'd be where I am if I wasn't stronger than breaking? I already know what it's like to be devoured by more pain than you could possibly imagine!"

A long silence throbbed heavily in the hot cell. Finally Bree cleared her throat and shook her head. "No Major, sir," she said quietly, "it's just . . . I'm not going to be able to watch Them do the same thing to you, I'm not. . . ." Her voice caught and she stopped speaking.

Skokes opened his mouth, but no words came out. Suddenly exhausted, he couldn't find the energy to speak. After what could have been minutes or hours, he found his voice. "You won't have to. Listen to me. . . . We're getting out. Because if we give up, it's over. Then Earth is gone, Mars is gone, the colonies: *gone*. They'll just wipe us away, take them for Themselves and there won't be anywhere left to go. There won't be any life left." The black obsidian rock face flashed before his eyes again and he watched, through the remembered fog of blood and pain, a Gila monster crawl over the rock pile of his mother's grave. *If I give in, it won't matter who's stronger. I had to pull myself back up to live.* "I have to get back into the fight. From now on our business is getting out of here, is that clear, soldier?"

She didn't say anything.

"I said, is that clear?"

She shook her head no.

Skokes started to grab her, but clenched his fists instead. "Dammit, if we lose, it's not just over for us, it's over for everybody!"

Bree trembled under his rage. "Yessir . . . whatever you say."

Women are the great warriors—they have endured, they have faced all. We owe them our lives. I have known this since my mother died for me, since my father wanted me to die for her. He felt terrible still thinking the thought that refused to leave his mind, but the words came out in spite of himself. "Where the hell did they find you?"

"I was drafted by the EDF. They introduced conscription for everyone over eighteen last year."

Skokes tensed, shocked. *How could they sacrifice like that? Is it the end? Are they really throwing the ones who gave us life to the aliens to fight?*

"You didn't know." Her response held no hint of a question.

He drew a breath. "I haven't been back to Earth in a long time."

She nodded slowly. "The war is everything now." Cocking her head to one side, she stuck her neck out and paused, watching him. "They came to my school and tested all of us. . . . They decided I had what it took to be a fighter pilot."

"They did, did they?" He couldn't help the sarcasm in his voice.

"I'm not what you expected from the 'greatest warriors,'" she lashed back. Her voice quavered, with fear or anger he couldn't tell. "I tried to be strong—you're right, I know . . . I told them they were making a mistake but they said the test results spoke for themselves."

How could such a terrible sacrifice be made for this war? How could she not be strong? Is she as weak as she seems? But he couldn't think too long about his conflict with her because it kept leading back to the old unresolvable family rage. He squatted and took several deep breaths, eyes closed, his fingers clenching and releasing around his lost hunting knife. When he finally opened his eyes, he felt cooler, calmer. He stood up.

Though her eyes were lowered, he felt Bree watching him. "Pretending to not look at me though your eyes burn with defiance is disrespectful," he said quietly. "You may as well—"

He stopped because she was already looking him directly in the eye before he finished the sentence. "I'm sorry," she said softly.

Now Skokes looked at the ground. "And I'm sorry I was so scared," she continued. He felt her reach for his arm. But he willed himself to stand there. She drew back. "I was sick all the time. . . . Then I thought if they could take me from a trainer right from the heart of our own solar system, the war must be over—"

Skokes fell several times as he struggled to reach the door. He threw himself against it, straining against the slimy, sharp rock face. "No!" The words ripped out of him as he yanked with all his might against the unmoving, unchanging stone. "We beat Them that day. They came right into our own back yard and for once we got mad enough for it to make a difference!" He was yelling to Bree, but turned his voice to the door, screaming at the jailer he knew waited on the other side. "AS A MATTER OF FACT, I PERSONALLY TOOK OUT THEIR CAPITAL SHIP! D'YOU HEAR ME OUT THERE!?! I'M NOT AFRAID OF YOU! I'VE KNOWN UGLIER THINGS AND I'M NOT AFRAID OF YOU!"

The sound of stones clicking underwater coincided with Bree's hand touching his shoulder. Skokes leapt back.

"There's nobody out there who can hear you." Her voice sounded sad.

Skokes gave up on the door. "No*body?* They're not human, They're nothing. No*thing.* That's what They are. No Thing." He moved towards one of the crevasse pools in the floor, pacing its edge like he might dive in.

"But you call Them They. Why?" Bree's question cut through the heat and damp like the prow of a canoe through a swamp.

Skokes shrugged, uncomfortable with the question, and went on as if she hadn't asked it. "It doesn't matter. It's important. It proved we could win. It was the first time we hurt Them worse than They hurt us." He paused, remembering coming to at the foot of his mother's grave, taking a jagged chunk of obsidian and slicing three cuts across the bruises his father had punched into his face, the hot flow of the blood from the top cut running into the blood from the second and down to the third. Then he placed the bloody rock on top of her tomb and turned to face his father, who leaned over, his hands on his knees, catching his breath after beating his son. Skokes smiled as he saw in his mind's eye the chaotic fear in his father's eyes when he realized his son's eyes wouldn't look away.

Bree smiled back. "Did it make a difference?"

Skokes jumped and nodded. His stomach lurched at her smile, and he wondered how she could be reading his thoughts. Then he realized she had to be responding to his earlier outburst. "It made Them change Their tactics, back off, keep Their Capital ships in the rear instead of committing Them. . . ." He wanted suddenly to be alone in the cell. "It gave us a standing eight count. . . ." *Eight again.* Distracted, he struggled to pick up his train of thought. "It made us realize They're not indestructible and it was time we found that out."

On his knees, Skokes plunged his arm deep into the clear water pool shaped like an undulating triangle. He peered through the bluish bulb light into the flotsam and jetsam. More of the hairy seaweed-like growth coated the walls of the pool. He reached for some, only to find it retracted under his touch. Repulsed but impatient, he grabbed at the floating "hair" and yanked out a fistful. He tried to throw it down, but it clung soft and slippery to his arm.

"Ugh!" He plunged his arm back into the water, thinking the stuff would drift off, but instead it seemed to entwine more securely around his arm. "And just at that moment, when I'm needed more than ever, just when I'm trying to defend a whole shipload of colonists trying to make it back to the Sol system...." He felt deeper. Nothing but black water, black hole. He stretched full out on his side, but the pool was much deeper than the length of his arm. Something rough and sharp grazed his wet skin and he flashed back on the textbook picture of the crocodile on the bank. He jerked his arm out of the pool. "I lost my main engine. One flight mechanic makes one stupid mistake calibrating a flow regulator and I'm out of the damn war!" The prickles of adrenaline making him nauseated, Skokes flung a handful of the wet muck against the ragged rock wall.

A door thudded open somewhere outside their cell. The heat intensified for a moment. Sweat poured off Skokes's face. "What was that?"

He started to move in front of Bree to protect her, but she slipped past him, her head tilted sideways to the right. "They come once a day with food," she said eagerly.

He moved in front of her again, arms out. "All right, stand back—"

"Please don't—" She pushed around him, her hands sliding down his arm, her eyes huge in the low light. Her head cocked to the left. The eye he could see fixed on the door, and her pupils slid open. He frowned.

The footfalls of the jailer approaching down the corridor grew louder. But Skokes crouched, still staring at the strange angle of Bree's head. He was caught off guard when the steam blast from the walls scalded him back into the center of the room. Gasping, he quickly crawled back to the door, but the jailer blasted the steam harder, and that, together with the pulsing pressure of the outside corridor, caused Skokes to pass out. He came to almost immediately when the jailer dropped a fist-sized creature right onto his face. Skokes yelped when crab-like claws tore into his moist, wrinkled facial skin as the creature raced to get away. Leaping into a war crouch, he held his fists in front of him, winking sweat and blood out of his eyes as he tried to locate the jailer.

The jailer tossed another of the creatures at Bree and blindly kicked Skokes in the belly as It lumbered out. The door slammed shut inches from his face and he pulled his hands back just in time.

Bree watched the creature nearest her, her head cocked again to one side, her pale eyes glutted with black. The grayish-blue organism, looking like a cross between a horseshoe crab with projecting fangs and a bloated scorpion, scuttled around in tighter and tighter circles before suddenly breaking its pattern and dashing to the wall, where Bree pounced on it. Squealing, its legs and pincers flailing, the creature snapped at the lure of wiggling fingers on Bree's left hand. Gripping it tightly in her right hand, she grabbed its head as it extended its knobby neck out of its round, protective shell, and twisted it off. Tossing the head and teeth aside, Bree threw back her head and tipped the round body to her mouth as if it was a bowl of soup. Jellied clots of black viscera leaked down her cheeks and neck as she slurped the contents of the body cavity.

Skokes slumped against the wall, gritting his teeth against his roiling stomach.

Bree stopped, still clutching the shell, and wiped away a string of chunky, purple intestine from the corner of her mouth. "This is all They give us." She pointed to the remaining creature, whistling and whirling about the cell. "Pretend it's snake meat or something. You've eaten that, haven't you?" The creature disappeared into the dark edge of the wall.

"I'm not hungry for Their food." He wiped his own mouth unconsciously, still looking at the dark smears on her cheeks.

She straightened, her glance moving from where the creature had disappeared to Skokes's face. "You have to keep your strength up. . . . It took the commander and me days to figure out it was supposed to be food." She gulped and cleared the watery rattle in her throat. Skokes barely repressed a gag. "It took me even longer to try to eat one." She crept toward the creature's hiding place, barely able to contain her excitement. "There's an easy way to kill them, I'll show you."

Skokes shook his head. "I saw."

Bree dropped her gaze again. "They're nearly tasteless as long as they're still warm. . . ." She hesitated, then smiled brightly. "I could catch it for you if you like." She sucked at the shell she still held.

Skokes held up his hand in the direction of the creature. "I'd rather starve, thanks."

Slurping at the dripping strings of entrails hanging from the shell, Bree scrabbled around at the base of the wall, feeling around with her free hand for the creature. After a minute or two, she stopped. "The commander said that. They waited until he *was* starving. That's when the torture started." Dropping the empty shell, she wiped her trembling hands on her suit. "They stopped bringing him food then." She paused, still facing away from him, her head angled back over her left shoulder. "They only fed me when he was gone. It didn't take very long until he was begging for mercy." She crouched low on the ground, reaching gently along the wall. "They understand our language, I think. They can speak it to us through this machine. But They don't seem to understand mercy. I don't think there's a word for it in Their language. Do you think that's possible?" She turned around to face him, wiping her mouth with the arm bearing the alien graft.

How could you let that thing touch your mouth? He stared at her and swallowed hard.

Bree seemed to realize what she was doing and jerked her head back, grimacing at her arm. "Do you think it's possible, since there isn't a word for mercy in Their language, that They don't know what it is? That for Them it doesn't exist?" She gasped and doubled over, cradling her arm to her belly. "Please eat."

How can I let this happen to her? I can't let her die. Raging at himself, Skokes spoke quickly, trying to distract her from the pain. "I'll either be gone or dead long before anything like that happens to me, you can stop worrying about—"

Bree cried out and spasmed again, burying her grafted arm under her other arm, and crossing both arms tight against her chest. "Do you think if They don't know what mercy means, it *can't* exist since it needs two?" She spoke between gritted teeth. "That it means nothing without two?"

"What? You're not making any sense." He went to her. "I can't understand you."

She held her ravaged arm gingerly, her greasy hair plastered against her head. "This one's taking so fast."

Skokes stopped. "What do you mean 'this one'?"

Bree winced and straightened her arm, breathing shallowly. "It's the third graft they've tried. They said—through the machine They said—They're looking for ways to overwrite the human DNA with Their own. . . . That's how They're changing me. Overwrite . . . changing the words, the meaning, me."

Skokes dipped his hand in the clear water pool, and held the liquid to his face. It smelled and felt like swamp water. He touched it to her face. "Why?" he said softly. Her face felt cooler than the water.

"They said it was an experiment." She grimaced. "It's working this time...."

"Let me see." Skokes took her arm.

Bree pulled it away and groaned. "It hurts."

This time, Skokes grabbed her arm. "Let me see," he said, frustrated. *I have to protect you.* He wrenched it up towards the glowing bulb. Bree yelped. "Maybe there's a way to scrape it off, cut it away, cut it out of you somehow—"

"NO!"

"What if this is only the beginning? What if They want to change all of us?" He turned his back to her, pinning her arm under his, holding her wrist straight so the graft faced up at him. "Hal-wuk! It is bad! We can't let them."

Bree beat at him with her other arm. "NO! DON'T!"

Skokes grabbed her forearm and dug his nails into the soft part of the placental growth between the furrows of scaly, horny triangles, into the white and purple bubbles, determined to snag one of the gluttonous blue-red veins and yank it out. "Close your eyes and bite down hard—"

She whiplashed her body against him so hard he almost lost his grip, bruising his ribs as he popped several of the soft bubbles. Hot, clear, viscous liquid spurted over both of them. Bree screamed, her mouth dark except for the rows of white teeth. The door flew open and Skokes was blasted by a face full of steam.

The jailer raced through the steam and grabbed Bree by the arm, dragging her out, her head clunking against the slimy rock floor.

Skokes tried to yell, but Bree had clubbed him in the chest so hard he could only gasp. "Hang on."

Bree grabbed his arm, kicking and screaming now against the jailer. "Please no, no, no!" Her fingers clawed at his forearm as her slender arm stretched to the point of breaking against the jailer's indifferent strength. The jailer yanked them both across the floor, forcing Skokes to release Bree as the door slammed shut, nearly cutting her in half. He threw himself at the door again and again, growling, raging.

The blue bulb went through countless cycles of burning brighter and dimmer as Skokes paced every corner of the cell, feeling into every crevasse. The algae-like substance littered the rock floor in wet, black clumps. As he searched, he ground his teeth until he gave himself a terrible headache, but he willed the pain back by biting on the striped, multi-colored headband he pulled off his neck. "Your cruiser didn't even know I was there until it was too late. I got off two mark nines . . . those nukes exploded five hundred yards away from Your main engines and You should've been there!"

He guffawed as he rinsed his hands in the water pool, trying not to think about Bree. Rubbing his eyes, he leaned back and sighed. After staring at the wall for a while, he noticed the algae he'd splattered against the wall earlier had begun to peel away. He walked over to the wall, pulled down a piece and rolled it into a section of rope. Yanking, twisting, pulling, he tested its strength and found it held. He peeled more of the dried vegetation off the wall, weaving it into a cord, talking the whole time so the jailer wouldn't get suspicious. "I could see maybe a hundred of Your bodies flailing from outside that ship and I fired my last ounce of propellant and took my fighter right through You—like bugs on a windshield. If I'd had the fuel I'd have done the same to every one of You!"

The rope was strong, and soon Skokes had twisted a lengthy piece of it. *Lop-fi-eets-chay! Let us hunt!* He smiled and kept weaving it, reveling in the remembered victory. "That cruiser broke up over Europa and I just sat in my cockpit with no fuel and watched You die for a change—and I'm gonna do it again, do You hear me? I'M NOT DONE YET, SO COME ON!" He stood near the ledge Bree had occupied and touched her filthy, blood-soaked outer flight suit. The stink of old blood shot up Skokes's nose, forcing him to look up. He stared at the triangular metal grate in the rock ceiling many feet above his head. Stripping down to his inner flight suit, he stood on the ledge where he'd first seen Bree lying down, dropped the rope and leapt for the grate. He jumped high but still nearly missed the bars and fell. He tried again. The fingers of one hand just grabbed the edge of the grate and he hauled himself up to the bars, groaning at the ache in his muscles and the friction on his burned, sliced skin.

Shaped like the underside of a pyramid, the grate offered just enough room for Skokes to pull his head up against the bars. He peered down the length of a passageway of the same ragged black rock as the cell. It was obviously some kind of air vent. The metallic clink of stones hitting against each other underwater echoed off the walls, vibrating Skokes's eardrums to the point where it was painful. He started to tear off a piece of cloth to plug his ears, but stopped when he realized he had to keep listening so he could tell where the sound originated from. Mixed in with the echo was the sound of scrabbling claws, but that disappeared after a moment or two.

The corridor stretched endlessly in either direction, periodically marked by other dimly lit "pyramids," probably other cells with other prisoners. *If I could get through these bars, I could get out. The corridor's big enough.* Skokes's arms quivered and he had to drop back into the room. *A way out.* He glanced at the flight uniforms on the ledge as he rubbed his trembling muscles. *For us.*

He walked around, testing the algae he was drying for more rope against the wall, then his fingers snagged on something sharp.

A section of rock in a natural seam revealed a knifepoint sliver of crystal that appeared as though it could be broken away. He tried to pound it free, but it only cut his fists. He needed something like a piece of rock to hit it and chip it loose. Half squatting, half crawling, he reached into the darkened areas for any chunk he could use as a tool.

The creature bit deep into his hand.

Skokes yelped and jumped back as the scorpion/horseshoe crab thing scuttled into the water pool. Wiping his arm on his suit, he took a few deep breaths and laughed. "It's not me you have to worry about." He stuck his arm back into the dark recess and his fingers closed on a loose chunk of black rock. He gave in to a controlled victory hoot before he took it over to the pointed sliver and began hammering away.

A dozen or so hits nearly exhausted him. He wasn't sweating anymore, as he hadn't drunk any water since his capture. He stopped, scooped a quick handful from the surface of the clear water pool and gagged it down. Returning to the sliver, he pounded it once more with all the strength he could summon up. A distinct CRACK and the wafer-thin black dagger of crystal fell into his hand. Whooping sotto voce, he ran it across his hand to try out its edge. Of course it drew blood easily in this damp atmosphere.

Chuckling at the fact that he'd tested it on himself rather than on the nearby cell wall, Skokes jumped back up to the ledge. He didn't know how much time he had before the jailer came back. His arms ached, but he focused all his concentration on pushing back the pain so he could hold himself up against the bars. Hardly daring to breathe, he drew the dagger across one of the crossbars. It cut deep into the metal beam.

Skokes yelped and strained to cut some more, but heard a sound from below and dropped back into the room, just in time to fall straight into another searing blast of steam. He shielded his already crunchy-burned skin as best he could from the blistering heat.

A body rolled into him. Bree, naked now except for her military issue undergarments, clawed her way over him, and he grabbed her and held her close. Her naked skin burned hot and slippery against his, and she stank of fresh blood and blistered skin. And underneath it, the cool, slightly marshy smell of the swamp. He supported her head in his arm as she fell back, barely conscious. Awkwardly Skokes slid backwards still holding Bree, and pulled his flight suit off the ledge to cover her.

"They've started. . . ." Bree croaked.

"What have They started?" Skokes tensed as she half slid, half crawled across his legs and buried her face in his lap. Again the textbook image of the twenty-foot crocodile flashed through his mind. Fascinated and horrified, he stared at the tiny incisions which dotted her limbs all along the meridian lines of her body. Each gash glowed firefly green while out of it pushed a scaly, triangular, reptilian carbuncle.

"Oh God," Bree gasped.

"It's all right." Skokes wanted to pat her shoulder but his hand felt frozen in place. His legs wouldn't move.

"They don't use anesthetic—"

Skokes watched the chitinous knobs pushing ever so slowly but purposefully out of her bruised skin and nodded. "I know." He spoke softly, and his hand began caressing her hair.

She groaned, burying her face in his lap. "It hurts so much. . . ."

"I know." He leaned down and kissed her head. She flinched and slowly turned her face up to his.

"Please hold me . . . Skokes."

"Nan-ces-o-wee." He smiled. "Nan-ces-o-wee." He stroked her cheek.

"What is that?" she asked, her voice barely audible.

"She was said to be the most beautiful Seminole squaw. The tribal elders offered her to a daring young brave named Ko-nip-hat-cho on the condition that he renounce his decision to go and learn from and live with the white man. He was warned to return to the tribe, he was threatened with Il-it, with death. But it was her terrible beauty that finally. . . ." His gaze kept traveling from her face back to the alien seeds in her skin. *I am a hadjo. I will be the great warrior for the greatest warriors.* He pulled her closer. "I want you to know something . . . Bree." He swallowed as her fingers slid around his waist, and down to clasp his hips. "I want you to think about this. When you were gone I found something that will get us out of here—"

"You did?" Bree's grip tightened and her face searched his. In this light, her pupils seemed to slide to slits. He blinked. They shrank to pinpoints, paling into clear pools of white or gray.

"Yes." He motioned for her to keep her voice low. "It will just take time—"

"I don't have any more time—"

"You have to be strong—"

"I don't know how much longer I'll be human."

He took her face in his hands and forced her to look right into his eyes. "You'll always be human. No matter what they do." He leaned closer, shielding her eyes from the light and the pupils slid lazily open, flooding her eyes with dark pools. "They'll never be able to change that. Ever."

Seeming to forget her shame, she reached up with her grafted arm. He started to pull his uniform over it, and she cringed.

"I won't hurt you again," he murmured and touched his lips to her sweaty forehead, catching, below the blood smell, a delicious, cool water scent.

Bree relaxed and the lines in her face smoothed. "You're wrong, you know."

"About what?" He stroked the hard, lumpy ridges of her grafted arm through the coat, wondering at its seductive familiarity.

"They can change us. We've been changing ever since the war started." Her voice was quiet.

"How?"

"You haven't seen it. Earth I mean. You've been out here."

"Here." He thought about it for a minute. "Space." *What did here mean? Where was the sun?* "Four years ago." He paused again. "Four solar years ago, I flew in the squadron that escorted the UN President back to Earth after he tried to negotiate the surrender of the Epsilon Colony." He swallowed. "Before They wiped it out. It was the last time I swam, the last time I ate meat . . . the last time I saw the sun against a blue sky."

"The last time you made love."

He caught his breath sharply and tensed. His face flushed. "I've never made love."

Her pupils opened wider, darker still as she stared into his eyes. Distinctly uncomfortable, he moved back, letting the bulb's light shine directly on her face again. Pale irises swallowed the blackness, water closing over an open maw. "Never? Why not?"

"Because...." He paused, shame and anger choking his throat. "Because I killed my mother in childbirth and because my father is right. I don't deserve a woman, having killed one of the greatest warriors with my own unproved life."

Bree's lips parted and he tensed, ready for a taunt, something. But when she spoke, it was about Earth. "You wouldn't recognize it now. Earth has changed so much in the last four years.... The war has changed everything."

Thank you for sparing me further shame. Skokes jumped in quickly. "They've woken up. They know what they're fighting for."

"What *are* they fighting for?" Bree sat up and the flight suit he covered her with slid off her, revealing a triple ridge of gray-brown and dull black tiny pyramids down an arm turned olive with bruises. "There are no more blue skies. Just the dull gray of acid fog belching from the munitions factories that work all through the night now. It's a police state of rationing and work; of fear and hate, and I *don't* miss it." She looked at the pain in his expression and sighed. "It's Germany or Japan in 1945." Bree touched his face with the hand that was still human. "It's the beginning of the end."

He shook his head. "No. You're wrong." And he remembered the sun peeping over the canyon walls, shining on their little family house in Nevada. The canoe rides through the Spanish-moss-strewn cypress swamps in O-kee-cho-bee long after his mother died and he'd left his father, before entering the Star Service.

"You haven't been there." Bree's voice held an edge.

Skokes got up, turning away so she wouldn't see where his arousal strained against his trousers. He shook his head, desire spinning and whirling his thoughts. His mind felt dizzy. The council's resentment of his achievements suddenly didn't matter anymore. "Before the war the Earth still hadn't come together as one world. We were a hundred different voices arguing in as many languages. But we were still and always had been one world with the same histories, the same things precious to us in any language." He turned back to Bree. "I know They can be beaten, Bree. I've done it. And as soon as the Earth Defense Force realize they *can* win, they *will* win. I believe that."

She looked at him, expressionless, before she suddenly turned amazed. "You do, don't you." It was a statement, not a question.

Skokes frowned at her instant mood change before finally smiling in spite of himself. *She's just been alone for too long.* "Yes." He helped her to her feet and held her at arm's length, searching her face for the conviction he felt so strongly. But he saw only puzzlement. "And at the end of the last battle," he persisted, "they'll be able to stop and look at themselves and remember *exactly* who they are. And *what* they are." He gripped her arms tightly, nodding at her grafted arm. "That they're *still human*." His voice caught, and he had to wait a minute before speaking again. "And so are *we*."

Something in Bree's face changed. Her eyes glittered.

He leaned in to kiss her, but she stretched out her neck and cocked her head sideways. Her chin jutted out as she jumped away from Skokes. The creature had crawled out of the water hole and Bree pounced. Clutching it tightly, she brought it back to Skokes, wrapping his swollen fingers around its oily carapace. "Take it."

He jerked back. "No." He tried to look thankful for her generosity. "You."

Bree shook her head and presented it again. "If you're going to find a way out of here, then you need your strength."

He smiled. "Your optimism gives me plenty of strength. But if you're coming with me, you need strength, too." Gently he pushed the creature and its snapping jaws back at her. Bree nodded reluctantly, then with a surprising show of strength, she twisted its neck, tore off its face, turned her back to Skokes and tilted back her head. Skokes averted his eyes. His erection diminished.

They took Bree again much later, but it was a controlled leave-taking for both of them this time, a glance exchanged to say she was one of the greatest warriors. Still he missed her terribly, for she was gone a long time, long enough for him to weave a rubbery chest harness from the dried vegetation. He hauled himself up to the bars, hooked the harness onto the highest remaining part of the metal pyramid and began sawing. He cut through three of them before he heard the telltale return thuds in the outside corridor. This time though, he barely had enough time to get down and ditch the harness, though he wondered why he bothered as the steam burned his swollen skin. All They seemed to care about was getting the door closed again as quickly as possible.

The most recent line of triangular scales had pushed up out of Bree's skin almost an inch now, their glowing verdant green turning a muddy brown. She sat watching him, back in the harness, sawing away at the bars. As he stopped to catch his breath and tried somehow to cool down, Bree made him gulp more water. It still tasted spore-laden, but otherwise seemed to be ordinary water.

At that moment, a human voice screamed from somewhere way down the air shaft. "Please stop! I don't know anything, please!" Then the sounds of grinding and lots of clicking stones under water. The voice screamed, "Let me die, please!"

Skokes quickly unhooked the harness, dropped to the floor, and knelt by the pool, splashing water on his face, hoping the water noise would drown out the screaming burned into his head.

Dressed in his flight suit, Bree watched him from her ledge. She'd had to roll up the arms and legs and through the unzipped top of the coveralls, he saw the curve of one breast. She crossed her arms and his gaze caught the raised seed scales. Skokes clenched his jaw. "Whoever he is," he muttered, looking up at the air shaft, "he should be stronger than that, a warrior—"

"Have you ever been tortured?" Her voice pointed sharply to what he'd said.

"I believe I have." He looked at her. "I've been beaten, burned, left for dead. I've been trained. I know in my heart that there's nothing They could do to make me give up my people." He met her gaze in the shadows. "What did They do to you?"

"Osceola was finally tricked by the Es-ta-had-kee, wasn't he?" she said, a strange pain in her voice.

"I won't make the same mistake," Skokes responded, more sharply than he intended. He avoided looking at her arm as he spoke for he found himself too sickened and too sad. "We—you can't let Them make you sick at heart."

Bree's eyes slid to her arm and she bit her lip. Another purple tentacle uncoiled from under the spreading reptilian skin and burrowed, foraging deep into her arm. Tilting her head back, Bree gasped and closed her eyes. Skokes's glance traveled from her arm to her white throat. His stomach felt heavy with nausea and desire.

"This is the worst thing They could've done. . . ." she whispered hoarsely. "But before, after we were here a day or so, They took the commander and me into another room and made us take off all our clothes. I was so ashamed. . . ."

Skokes's mouth went dry. He swallowed hard as he caught himself staring at her slender torso. Bree stooped to sit down and her breasts pressed heavily against the thin, dirty, khaki material of her undershirt. Skokes coughed and looked away.

Bree continued, shivering out her words. "They didn't spend much time looking at the commander but I don't think They'd ever seen a woman before because They—" she made a sound that was half like a laugh, half a gulping hiss. Skokes found himself looking at her again. Her eyes glowed in the darkened corner. *The greatest warriors.*

"Two others came in—smaller, like we are—I guess They were females. . . ." She bit her lip. "And They examined me inside. And then a voice—a machine voice—asked me if I was a warrior." She leaned out of the dark, motionless except for the rise and fall of her breasts.

Skokes stared, hypnotized, into her eyes. *The greatest warrior.*

"Like the man. I said I was just a cadet, I didn't know anything about the war. I only knew what they'd told me about the Exeter fighter: thrust to mass ratios, Delta V." She withdrew into the darkness. "It was all I knew, but I told Them."

Skokes took a deep breath and shook his head. "It's all right . . . They've captured enough of our Exeter fighters to know them by heart."

Bree got up. Again came the sound of stones hitting underwater. She glanced towards the door before he did. After a moment, Bree continued. "They thought the commander knew important things—defense secrets—because of his rank. He was trained too, but—I don't think he knew anything. He was hurt in the first year of the war. I don't think they tell instructors defense secrets." Her voice softened. "Do they?"

"No." Skokes went to her. Her back was turned.

"He just wanted it to end. We were going to commit suicide but he was too weak and I was too—"

Skokes reached around and covered her mouth before she could get the word out. He pressed up against her in one motion, hunting her as his father had taught him, as his mother had taught his father. "Don't say it," he hissed in her ear. The cool smell of her sweat made him thirsty and he found himself about to lick her neck. She pressed back against him as he ground his hips against her bottom. He spun her around and took her by the shoulders, letting his thumbs run along the full curve of her breasts. She seemed to be watching him, breathing rapidly, her mouth open, just the tip of her teeth showing. Dizzy with desire, he shook his head, and laughed. "What did I tell you? Hm?"

She grinned back. "That you're going to find a way out of here."

He frowned, trying to look stern, all the while the smile twitching at the corners of his mouth. He felt hot, but good somehow. "What else?"

She jutted her neck out to the side again and looked out at him from one eye. The stance at that moment chilled him. "You're not leaving without me." She grinned again.

"Damn right," he said, although this time he forced the gusto. He glanced back at the grate. Bree groaned and reached around her back, scratching. Skokes heard a sound like when his father cleaned the scales off the garfish they'd caught during their trip to visit his mother's kin. "Does it hurt?" he said, trying not to grimace.

She shook her head. "Not anymore. . . . Not like before. . . ." She went on scratching. Goosebumps rose on Skokes's arms and legs despite the cave's heat. "It feels strange. I can't see what They've done back there. . . . Would you?"

She'd turned away from him, but had he heard the slightest challenge in her voice? He hesitated a moment. "Please?" Her voice was quiet.

He nodded, even though she couldn't see him, and stepped up behind her. She slid the flight suit off her shoulders and crossed her arms across her chest. The outer side of her breasts pressed curves in her chest's silhouette. Skokes's eyes widened as they moved from her breasts to her back.

Her spinal column, which should have been hidden, appeared to have been peeled into three strips, like bark. The triangular knobs pushed slowly up against her bruise-darkened skin. Lines striped her back horizontally between the three ridges of her spinal cord at one-inch intervals, forming squares of leathery, dark scales. Even as he looked, new pyramids pushed against her skin, like misshapen fetuses struggling against the sacs that held them.

Skokes retched silently as he reached out and touched her back. "It looks fine," he lied.

Bree flinched at his touch, and he came closer as he moved his fingers gently across her back, hoping somehow to comfort her. "I'm sorry," he said finally.

She glanced over her shoulder and smiled gamely before turning away again. "It's all right. I told you it would be like this. You had to know."

He stopped, his hands clenched into fists. *How could we let this happen to her? How could I let this happen to her?*

"Please don't stop," she said, "I'm just not used to being touched like that."

"No?" he said, surprised. A strange thrill twitched in his stomach.

"You're forgetting how much Earth has changed," she reminded him.

"I don't understand . . ." he stammered, feeling like she had eyes in the back of her head. *How can she see what's happening in me?*

She waited for him to continue his gentle rubbing of her shoulders before she went on. "All the boys over the age of sixteen are sent to the Defense training program. . . . The commander was the only man in my squadron so . . ." she gulped and trailed off.

"Never?" The words rushed out before he could stop himself and his erection swelled hard with a heavy ache. He tried to shift his position and keep his touch moving across the gritty scales to where her skin was still human, but his damp hands caught on the triangular ridges, opening the skin on his palms like a seam. He drew a sharp breath. She started to turn around but he moved so as to still stand behind her.

She nodded. "It's true. You're the only man—other than my father when I was very young—who's ever touched me like you're touching me now." She sighed and gave the strange laugh that was like the cry of some marsh creature. "You'll be the last, too, because it won't be very long before I won't be human at all." She shivered violently.

Skokes pulled up the baggy flight suit to cover her reptilian shoulders, but when he reached them, she stopped him, covering his hands with her own. "Please." The blood in her hands pulsed with the temperature of the cell; still her fingers felt cold.

He moved closer and dropped the cloth, pressing his body against hers and still holding himself apart as much as he could. She leaned into him and he closed his eyes, fighting the urge to put his lips to the cool skin just under her jaw where it met her neck.

"Bree," he whispered and started to get up, "I should get back to work."

Bree stopped him, turning to embrace him. "Can we sit like this just a little longer?"

He settled back into his position, his stomach twitching and his head spinning. Bree turned into him, lying across his lap, and the curve of her breast brushed across his lap. He drew a sharp breath and clenched his jaw so he wouldn't groan. His head fell back and he looked up toward the bars he'd been sawing through.

Bree's eyes were still closed. "If you get inside the vent . . . do you really think you'll find a way out?"

Skokes tried to move his hips away from her, but she nestled down further against him. The ache was unbearable. He tried to focus on the job of getting out. "Once I'm through the bars I'll be able to scout every day for a few hours. I mean, if They were really listening, They'd have stopped me by now, wouldn't They. That's Their overconfidence."

Bree's eyes opened wide and her pupils dilated into starless black. She leaned up close to his face.

"And when I find a way out of here, I'll cut away on that end like I'm doing here."

"And then?" The sound of stones clicked underwater once, but neither one of them turned to the door. Skokes stared at her a moment before his gaze tore away to look up again.

"Find a weapon. We know They bleed like we do." Frustrated, he slid out from under her, and shook his fists in the air. "Yo-ho-e-hee!" The war cry pierced the air of the cell. Bree's eyes darkened, and her muscles tightened. Skokes wiped a streak of blood across each cheek. "It just takes a helluva lot more to make Them do it." He whooped again, and danced three steps on one foot, then three steps on the next. Each time he ended by leaping into a watchful crouch. "Then we steal a ship. I flew one of Their scoutships that crash-landed near Base Eisenhower, so I figure with any luck I could fly us off this rock and back into human space." He crouched, trembling from the heady mix of desire, excitement and fear. "At least, we could kill a few of Them trying, right?"

Bree sat up tall and drew her arms in. She stared at him intently. "Would it be enough for you? Just to hurt Them?"

He shook his head and leaped again, his muscles still twitching. "Not enough, no. Let's just say it's the least I'll settle for."

She looked at him sideways. "You hate them that much." Her voice was strange; her whole attitude toward him now distant.

He stared at her and shook his head. "Look what They're doing to you. How can you ask me that?" He shook his fists in four directions, struggling with alien light and the ragged curves of the room to feel for and find the four corners.

"I just don't believe in hating anyone."

Skokes grabbed her by the shoulders. "Ho-lo-wa-gus. No good. Then try."

She threw off his hands, and got right in his face. "Why?"

Anger burst out of him. "I can give you a hundred reasons! For slaughtering the first ships we sent out to make contact with Them; for wiping out whole colonies of innocent people; for refusing to negotiate; for refusing our surrender—you go ahead and hate Them because it's the only emotion that'll get us out of this!"

"Not love?" She stared into his eyes and he felt his stomach drop. His ears buzzed and his neck prickled. He swallowed and his mouth fell open. She touched his cheek, wiping away the war blood, and sucked it off her finger. He took a deep breath, and smelled the cool, murky water scent of her body. "I think that's just as important. More. It's what makes us different from Them, it's what defines us." Her face with its high cheekbones and dark eyes, the firm set of her mouth, was a warrior. "We have to fight for what we are. Don't we? Isn't that what you said?"

Skokes's hands clenched into fists, but they didn't last long. There was no tremble in her lip now. He glanced at her arm, scaly brown-black now criss-crossed with lines like a lizard. "Yes," he said finally, "I just haven't felt anything but hate for a long time."

Bree took his hands and placed them back on her shoulders. "I haven't felt *anything* for a long time." She looked into his eyes. His face grew hot. Flush spread up her cheeks. "When I was a kid, before the war, I imagined I felt love. At least, I imagined the feeling of being in love without ever having been. I imagined I would marry a man who loved me," her eyes grew big, "and we'd hunt together, and bear children together. And I imagined," she made a low rumbling in her throat, "making love would be the most wonderful feeling." Her eyes stayed on his as her lips just touched his. His skin tingled. "Is it?" she whispered, a tease in her voice.

Skokes pulled her closer, his eyes moving from her eyes to her lips, to her shiny, white teeth. "Yes," he whispered back hoarsely, hardly aware of what he was saying, "it is."

"I always thought one day I would know." Her breath seemed to flow into his open mouth like cool, sweet water. He wanted to drink her.

"You will." He closed his eyes and pulled her mouth to his.

But she jerked away. "Not if They keep changing me." She released him and yanked down her ragged flight suit, frustration and pain reddening her face.

Her breasts swung free of the thin undershirt, round and full, her nipples erect, the aureoles soft, tongue-pink.

"Bree . . ." He wanted to bite them until she screamed. His knees trembled with the effort of standing up.

"I still feel human. I still have all those feelings inside, I just don't have any more time. . . ." She pointed to the meridian lines of pyramid-shaped scales spreading across her chest and arms, the greenish glow racing like liquid firefly along the cracks between the scales. Her eyes didn't look at him. "Would you hold me again? I just want to feel that much. What a man's body feels like against mine. While it's still mine. . . ."

Skokes grabbed her, but her scaly right arm rasped his skin raw. Instantly, Bree covered her breasts and went back to her ledge.

Skokes rubbed his eyes and groaned. He tried to apologize, but the words died in his throat. He went to her and tried to turn her head to look at him. But she wouldn't. "Look at me."

But she refused; instead she dragged the nails on her human hand across the scales, ripping and slashing at them until she drew blood. "It's not fair!"

He grabbed her hand and checked her arm. No damage there, but blood poured from her broken fingernails. "Don't." He pulled her to him, feeling her heart beat with the heat of the room.

"You know what I am," she whispered just below shouting. "You know what I am—you don't want to touch me—"

"That's not true—you're beautiful! Nan-ces-o-wee!"

She shook her head harder and harder, lashing it back and forth. "No, I'm not, not now—"

"Now! Right now, you are!" He crushed her mouth on his and felt blood on his lower lip as she bit him. He yanked down her flight suit and dragged his tongue along her jaw, tasting blood and cool, murky water. It was all he could do to keep himself from tearing into her throat. They struggled to get off what remained of their clothes and he buried his face in her breasts, thrusting himself against her again and again even as she tore at his clothes. His tongue slid into her mouth, across her teeth, tasting the inside of her mouth, gulping the coolness in huge swallows.

Hot steam blasted from the walls, searing their naked flesh. Skokes roared as he came inside her, flooding her with his seed, not knowing if their own bodies or the blast hurled them into the rock wall, burning their skin. He moved over her, taking the brunt of the hideously hot water, his thirsty throat jerked away from the cool of her and yelled, "DON'T YOU TAKE HER!"

But the jailer's arm had already lifted him from her with that unconcerned, monstrous force. Skokes felt himself hauled out of her, and he cried out as her face disappeared into the hot mist, her eyes wide, her mouth open, screaming, "JOHN!"

He leapt to his feet, but fell, his pants dangling around his knees. Cursing, he scrambled to his feet, yanking them up and dove for the door, but it had already slammed shut.

Alone in the room, the intense heat dissipating to sweaty humidity, he forced his passion down by kneeling and crossing his fists against his chest. But his body shuddered with the echo of Bree's screams. As they grew further away, the stillness filled him with cold. *I drank from the Greatest Warrior, and I owe her my life and our children's lives.*

He grabbed his crystal dagger buried in the crevice, dug out his harness from where he'd thrust it under the outer layer of his flight suit and leapt up to the grate, pulling himself up the seven or eight feet effortlessly. Quickly he hooked himself to the bars and sawed at them until his arm ached. Flexing his other hand a moment, certain he heard Bree scream again, Skokes began sawing as hard as he could with his other hand.

Anytime his hands or arms ached too much to continue, he imagined the obsidian rock pile, the sun shining, cooking his bruises, his father whistling as he went about feeding the cows and sheep, and the sideways tilt of the lizard's head, its beady black eye watching him from a rock just above the ground. A buzzard wheeled and croaked somewhere in the sky above him. *I'm still alive and I'm still myself. They can't touch that. This is just another place with different pain.*

Hours or no time had passed when the algae rope harness crackled, crunched, and snapped. Skokes jumped when he hit the ground, as though he'd fallen asleep and been jarred awake, but he quickly leapt back on Bree's ledge and jumped for the grate once more. Holding on with a spasming left arm, Skokes sawed the dagger back and forth and through the last millimeter of metal. Gasping and laughing, he let his head drop back and swallowed the war whoop rising in him. He listened for the sound of stones clicking underwater. Hearing nothing and overwhelmed with exhaustion, he placed the dagger between his teeth, gripped the pyramid of bars with his right arm and pushed as hard as he could. It squealed upward and crashed to the side, landing on the rock floor of the tunnel just above his line of vision.

Just as he got his arms to hoist him up into the air shaft, his right hand gave out and sent him sliding down again. His fingers locked around the bar near the hinge of the pyramid, and he flailed, dangling just above his prison cave. Gritting his teeth so hard around the dagger his jaw ached, he dragged his body up and through the opening. His bleeding fingers numbly gripped for any hold, and he pulled himself onto the dirty, ragged sharp rock floor. Collapsing, he refused to even let out a single groan at the pain in his teeth when he released the dagger.

As he lay there panting, something scuttled around behind him in the passageway. Instantly he flipped over and crouched on all fours, facing the sound. It was too dark to see much past his own cave opening. The only light in the passageway came from the organic bulb in the cell. Peering into the dark, Skokes could just see the glow of another pyramid grate in either direction, underlit by the same bluish-green light as his own. He knelt and reached up carefully, trying to feel the height of the air shaft, but he couldn't quite straighten his arms. He started crawling toward the sound. The scrabbling feet returned, closer and faster, but the echo in the corridor made it impossible for him to determine which way they were coming from.

Something slammed into his back with such force his arms flew out from under him. He fell flat, hitting his jaw, and blacked out. Coming to instantly or a long time later, he found his face ripped raw as whatever the monster was dragged him along the sharp, ragged ground. Grunting each time his swollen jaw bumped against the jagged rock, Skokes managed to turn his head around and saw he was passing the pyramid to his cell. His mangled fingers locked around the edge of the open grate. The claw grip tightened and sharp teeth tore into his right calf.

He cried out and the thing bit him deep into the same wound. His other hand found his dagger. Kicking as hard as he could at the monster behind him, he reached for the bars closest to him. With a snarling gobble, it yanked him back. He pulled again, managed to switch arms, locked the fingers of his other hand around the grate, and swung the dagger back and down. He groaned as his shoulder popped out of joint, but the adrenaline drove him to stab and stab into the formless black mass chewing into his leg.

A long, gurgling shriek met his first thrust. . . . *Snake meat. You've eaten that, haven't you?* Bree's words echoed in his head, and he pictured his arm transforming into a snake striking again and again with the knife. The creature squealed, finally retreating with the scuttling and scrabbling that Skokes kept hearing all around him and so kept stabbing at it long after it had gone. His head throbbed and his jaw was so swollen he couldn't move it. Slowly he pulled himself up to a sitting position, but kept passing out as he sat over the grate, gripping the bars with one hand to swing himself down. Realizing he would fall if he only used one arm, he grabbed his shoulder. "One," he groaned, hardly able to form the word, and jerked it back into place. The pain turned the blackness white and he fell through the opening, only holding on with the one arm, smashing his bloodied leg against the ragged roof of the cave cell. Tears of pain streamed down his face as he reached with his numb shoulder to close the grate, but his other arm trembled uncontrollably.

Hundreds of clicking stones underwater. The jailer was coming back. Skokes pictured the black rock and the last kick from his father—the one that exploded his chest—and hauled himself up to the grate, grabbed the pyramid by the hinge and slammed it shut. But his fingers caught in the hinge and he had to let go in order to keep them from breaking. He fell to the floor, his wounded leg twisting under him. The dagger flew out of his mouth and skittered across the floor to the edge of the second crevasse pool, the one filled with dark, murky liquid and rimmed by giant white crystals. Skokes reached for it when the steam blasted his legs with such force and heat that he convulsed. Through sparkling stars of pain, he watched the dagger slide into the pool. He squeezed his eyes closed. *I'm still going to get out of here. I'm still alive. Earth is still alive. We were never conquered.*

He opened his eyes. Through the dissipating steam, the outline of the giant alien blotted out the entrance to the room. The metallic tinkling of stones, then It tossed Bree against him. The rock doors grated closed.

Bree moaned and clutched her arms to her chest. One was heavily bandaged. Skokes crawled over to her and gently took her in his arms. Bree still wore the outer layer of his flight suit, but now it was unbuttoned almost to her belly. She stank of rotting marsh.

Leaning her against his better arm, Skokes winced as he peeled back her sleeves. The liquid firefly glow had darkened to swamp green, black in places. Poking out of her skin almost three inches at their largest, the old ridges had hardened. New triangular scales twisted in the growing number of placental white-gray bubbles. Swollen red and blue tendrils mapped her limbs, foraging in all directions. Where the scales hadn't yet developed, her skin had begun to crust and flake, oozing pale yellow fluid.

"Ree? Ree. . . ." He couldn't make the sound of the "b" without pain knifing his jaw. She groaned. Something stuck into his stomach as he leaned over her. He felt along her torso. Hard ridges. He slid the flight suit all the way off her chest. Her breasts had all but disappeared into a mosaic of brownish-black ridges and triangles jutting out of her chest bones, the points of which had flattened and grown together in places. Only her nipples remained, but they had turned bruise purple with tiny purple-black veins climbing around them like strangler vines, pulling them into the morass of parasitic scales.

Skokes slowly covered her up again, his face as neutral as he could make it. Bree turned her face to him out of the tangle of her hair, and opened her eyes. The pupils slid open and black flooded her eyes to the point of pushing the irises into the sclera. Her cheekbones jutted out as though They had attempted to mold her face by pulling and squeezing it forward. Her smile seemed like a grimace with a pronounced under bite, almost as though They'd broken her jaw and extended it out. A single, neon-green dotted line ran down her forehead and nose. As Skokes pushed the hair from her face, tiny pyramids pushed through the surface of her skin and the line darkened.

Bree squeezed her eyes shut and turned her back to him. "Please don't look at me. They're making me a monster."

Skokes kissed her nose along the line of dots. The slow twist and throb of the dot as it pushed a ridge through the skin poked his lips. He forced himself to keep his lips there. "Never," he said, "You are the greatest warrior."

He ran his finger under her eye, stopping the tear before it started. For some reason, that depressed him terribly and his heart ached. "You were gone so long this time," he said quickly, eager to say something, anything, to get away from the pain in his heart. "Do you hurt?"

"Not like before." She tried to smile. "They must have a higher tolerance for pain than we do. This new skin," she rapped on her chest, making a hollow cracking noise like a rock hitting against an empty shell, "hardly feels anything." She frowned as she looked at him. "What's happened to you?"

Skokes nodded towards his mangled leg. "I ran into something with rather long, sharp teeth."

Bree sat up and slid the baggy flight suit over her scaly torso, and held it closed with her unbandaged hand. Slowly, she lifted herself off Skokes. Angry red and purple burns splotched the swollen skin around the ragged bite. Black lined the torn skin, and blood mixed with steam dripped on the floor. She reached out and seemed to notice for the first time that her other arm was heavily bandaged. She cocked her head from side to side, examining it until Skokes covered the bandage with his hand and took her arm. She looked at him and he shook his head.

She nodded and covered his wound with her unbandaged hand. He flinched and yelped, but after the initial pain, her touch cooled and soothed his ripped, seared skin. Blood ran out from under her fingers. Skokes ripped a piece of thin, plastic coolant hose from the body layer of his flight suit and tied it around his leg as a tourniquet. He frowned as he did, remembering the dagger sliding into the other pool.

"What did that?" Bree interrupted his thoughts.

"I never saw it. It was something in the air vent."

Bree laughed, excited. "You made it into the air vent?"

Surprised and cheered by her laugh, Skokes looked sheepish. "Yeah, then I got stupid. First the che-she, the rat in the maze," he walked over to the drain as he spoke, "then I lost the piece of crystal I was using to cut the bars down in this pool." Still looking at Bree, he stuck his arm past the salt-like crystals straight down into the black pool.

Acid scorched his arm, eating into his skin instantly. Skokes cried out and yanked his arm back so quickly he fell and slammed his head against a nearby rock. Bree was at his side in an instant. "You're hurt—"

Discombobulated and dizzy, he jerked away from her touch and heard the stones clinking together underwater. The staccato rhythm bit into his head. "Not yet," he muttered, dragging himself over to the detritus pool. His arm sizzled as he plunged it into the water up to the shoulder, gagging at the rotted, sweet-smelling smoke of fried flesh. "Hi-lit-la-ma-es-chay! Fire water . . ." he gasped after he finally caught his breath. Bree looked at him and shook her head, her hand to her mouth. "Acid—there's some kind of acid down there—" He sucked in quick shallow breaths against his teeth, twitching from the cool cold of the water burning against the scalding cold of the acid. "I cut my way into the vent, but without that crystal, I can't cut my way back out!" He yanked his arm out of the water. Dragging his sore leg behind him, Skokes stumbled over to the wall and started searching for another cutting tool.

Cool stung his mangled arm. He looked down to find Bree's mouth on the worst part of the seared flesh. The cool water sensation trickled down his torso, pooling in his groin, filling him, warm and heavy. He groaned under the weight of pain and desire.

Al-la-paw-taw. The word flashed into his mind, a caption under the textbook picture of the crocodile. *But it's not an alligator, it's the wrong word. It's a crocodile.* "Can't lose my head," he gasped, "got to stop. Lop-fi-eets-chay. Let us hunt." He thrashed and slid down the wall.

"Shh, you're hurt," Bree said, her head lowered so he couldn't see her face. He took a deep breath. His arm, where her lips had touched it, felt numb. His fingers kept grasping for another fragment of sharp rock. "John, you should rest."

"I found one, there could be another," he responded dully, trying to breathe the pain out of his head. He tried to war whoop as he forced his burned hand into all the possible crannies in the cave walls, but all that came out was a gasp.

"We have to bandage your leg, it could get infected . . ." Bree pleaded.

Skokes whirled around. "Be O-pa-na-ki-tee! Be a silent person!"

Bree still knelt, her hands folded palms up in front of her, her face still down.

"I'm sorry," he whispered after a minute, "I'm sorry, I just—my father would have beaten me for what I just did to you, and I would deserve it."

Bree looked up, her eyes glittering with tears. Skokes groaned and threw up his hands, yelping. "Ho-lo-wa-gus! No good! There's no good in bandaging my leg unless we can get out, Bree! There's no point in doing anything—anything!"

"I'm sorry," Bree said quietly.

But Skokes had already gone back to hunting the rock walls, digging into the moss. "That thing in the vent . . . I think I killed it. I'm sure it's dead. I can go back and find our way out if I just find something else to cut with." Behind him, he heard the tearing of cloth, a sticky peeling back of material. But he refused to turn around. Instead, he dug into the original crevice where he'd found the first crystal dagger. "I always carry my sa-lof-ka-fots-kee, my hunting knife, everywhere—how could I have let go of it after the crash? They weren't even looking to see that I had any weapons—how could I be so stupid?" He pounded at the crevasse, punctuating each word, ignoring the pain. *I lost my mother's hunting knife.* He pounded harder, against the horror of the loss.

"John?" Bree's voice trembled. Skokes turned around, hardly daring to hope that she'd found something.

Bree was kneeling at the edge of the acid pool, and had reached down into the hole up to her armpit. The bandages from her arm lay in a dirty heap next to her. "I can reach it." Her voice shook, but she seemed excited though clearly stunned. "I think I can touch it."

Skokes stood where he was, his mouth open. The image of the crocodile basking on the dried river bank flashed through his head again. *Al-la-pa-taw. No, not alligator, that's not the right word, why can't I think of the right word? Am I going mad?* He shivered, pushing the thought away. *Women are the greatest warriors.* "Bree, that's acid," he said, surprising himself with his calmness.

Bree turned to him, her eyes wide. "I have it." She was quivering all over.

Skokes squatted next to her and touched her shoulder. "Get it up, get your hand out of there now."

Bree rolled back on her knees, hesitated a moment, then turned to Skokes and pulled her arm up slowly to avoid splashing the acid. Skokes stared wide-eyed at the dagger gripped in what had once been a human hand. "I wish this could be your mother's sa-lof-ka-fots-kee, John."

He stared at the chitinous, black, ridged reptilian skin, tipped with long, curved silvery claws. "It will suffice," he said quietly. Something about what she just said bothered him, but he couldn't figure out what. The image of the crocodile flashed through his mind again, confusing him as he tried to figure it out, staring at the skin whose purple veins slithered beneath the scaly flesh. The claws came up close to his face, so close the acid steam stung his eyes. But Skokes stared directly at her through his watering eyes and took the dagger. His other hand reached out and caressed her face. She gasped and collapsed into him, and they tumbled to the ground and rolled away from the acid pool.

Hearing the stones clinking together underwater, Skokes prepared to shield her from the aliens coming in, but was lost in drinking down her bitter coolness as he slid into her darkness.

John stands in the alien cave. His mother's grave of obsidian rock lies where the acid pool should be.

His mother crawls up onto the grave on all fours. "There's no word for crocodile."

"What?" John says. "I have to watch your lips move because I've never heard your voice."

"I said there won't be enough room." She picks at the mound of her grave. "Here," she says something else that looks like "use this" but he stops watching her lips move because something bites his arm and the pain makes him look away for a minute.

"What did you say?" he says, trying to hear her over the noise of the bite.

But she's already thrown one of the rocks at him and it hits him in the chest.

Skokes jumped. Bree shook him gently. "John, what's al-la-pa-taw?" she whispered. She leaned up to look at him. "And what's Chit-ta-mic-co?"

Skokes blinked and raised himself on his elbows. "Where'd you hear that?"

"You kept saying that while we were making love." She kept her gaze steady on him, her head cocked to one side. Her eye rolled around to look at him. He swallowed hard. "You said it again in your sleep."

Upset and nauseated by the nightmare, Skokes had to wait a bit before he could talk. The pain in his head made him want to vomit. Dry heaves shook him. Bree brought him more water as soon as they abated. "Chit-ta-mic-co," he said when he could trust himself to talk, "is Seminole for Chief of Snakes and al-la-pa-taw is alligator—" He caught himself, seeing the look on her face. "No, Bree, I'm sorry, I didn't mean it against your body—please...."

Bree pulled her alien arm into the long sleeve of Skokes's flight suit. "It's okay, John," she said softly, "you're right."

"No," he said, trying to make her take the jacket off again, "I mean it's hideous, but you're not, it's ... anyway, neither of those words are right ... oh God, how do I explain this? I—my mind's jammed on this image of a crocodile and I keep thinking what's the Seminole for it and I keep coming up with alligator, which isn't the same thing and...." He blushed.

Bree clapped her hands. The claws made a skitchery sound. "There! Now your color's coming back. You'd turned so white, like a dead fish."

He laughed and winced. "This isn't exactly a normal situation, this first time lovemaking in a cave to a woman who's being experimented on here in some alien world after crashing and being jumped by one of Them."

"You don't have to be nice," she said turning away from him.

He grabbed her, groaning at the sudden pain in the leg that Bree had bandaged. "Being nice?" He laughed again. "I'm not. I'm being totally honest."

She turned back to him. But her eyes still looked sad even though she smiled. "So you were saying before about it only making us stronger in the long run?"

Skokes motioned for her to help him sit up without too much pain to his leg. He gazed at her and his heart ached. "I never thought. . . ."

"Yes?" she said after a minute, still holding his leg.

"Forget it," he said, suddenly feeling his father's kick in his ribs again. "What did you ask me?"

She studied him for a minute before returning to her original question. He thought back to when they'd been discussing the Great War. "The greatest warrior," he said softly. In brightening light from the bulb growth, Bree's eyes paled as the black drained out of them. Skokes shivered as he remembered her scaly arm rising out of the acid, gripping the sliver of rock that was the key to their freedom. "It'll only make us stronger in the long run. We'll be one race. Without all the noise that went on before the war . . . between countries . . . between Earth and Mars . . . between everyone. Hal-wuk, it is bad. But we'll have looked into the abyss . . . braced our backs against the howling wind, and chosen not to fall. Perhaps then," he tipped her face to his and frowned, "perhaps then, we'll have truly given back to the greatest warriors who gave us life."

Bree's eyes grew bright, and she ran her claws down his face, slicing into the old scars on his cheek. "Oh no, John, I didn't mean to, I forgot about them, oh no," she murmured. He shook his head, and they lay back.

"Home," she said at last, but her tongue stumbled over the word.

"Where?" Skokes asked. He turned and searched her face, trying to see into her eyes. "Where is your home?"

"In the heartland," she said finally with great effort. Again, she stumbled over the words. "When I was growing up, I could stand out on the porch and watch the wind whip through fields of alfalfa. . . . Forever. . . ."

Skokes caressed the sharp ridges of her arm, still hidden under his flight jacket, letting his fingers play along the points of the long claws at the end of what had been her hand. Bree pulled her arm deeper into his jacket. Her nails caught in the soft, wrinkled flesh of his fingertips, splitting them open.

Skokes winced and sighed, closing his wounded fingers against his palm. "When we get back—after the doctors reverse what They've done to you—I'd like to take you to a place where my mother's people live. It's on this freshwater lake called Kiss-imm-eé." He smiled remembering the mirror of water, the mist rising off it on those mornings before the temperature rose to ninety-five all at once. "There were still fish there four years ago." He shook his head and sighed. "Four years? What's that here? Forty? Fourteen? Oh well. There probably still are fish, it's pretty out of the way—even from all this. . . ." He smiled wryly and kissed her forehead. "And on a cool summer night we'll go out in a canoe—"

"And swim," Bree chimed in, excited.

"Yes." Skokes kissed her again. "Under the stars—"

"Promise me—" Bree seized his shoulders and looked right into his eyes.

He took her hands in his and squeezed until her claws cut into his palms. "I promise."

"And you won't have to feel hate anymore," she continued, her eyes searching his.

The sound of stones clicking underwater intensified and his head felt as if he was drowning. He swallowed hard against the ache in his heart. His ears suddenly popped as the door to the cell opened.

Skokes struggled to his feet, thrusting Bree behind him. The jailer stepped just inside the door and tossed two more squealing creatures at them. It stepped out again and the door slammed shut.

But Bree had already leapt out from behind Skokes and grabbed for the monsters as they attempted to scurry up the cave wall. She seized one and trapped the other, motioning for Skokes to come and pick it up. Halfheartedly, he took it, gripping it in both hands just as she had hers. They stood, facing each other. Skokes frowned. "They didn't hit us with the steam."

Bree gave no sign of having heard him as she eagerly readied the snapping-jawed, squealing head in her grip. "Let me show you how to do this."

"Why didn't They?" he persisted to himself.

Bree held the creature in her alien hand and twisted its head off in one motion with her human hand. "It doesn't take much pressure."

Skokes swallowed and followed her lead, tossing the creature's dripping head into a corner.

Bree cocked her head and stared at the food, her mouth slightly open. Her eyes rolled forward. "Like this," she croaked. She tilted her head back and dumped the contents of the creature's shell down her throat, gulping so fast some of the entrails backwashed out of her mouth and down her neck. As they did, she snapped at the escaping mouthful, spraying viscera and body fluids.

Skokes tried to follow suit, but seeing Bree triggered the gag as the sour entrails started down his throat and he retched them out again. "God, that's awful," he gasped, bent over.

Bree's alien arm shot out and rescued the mouthful before it hit the ground. Her mouth was open to take it when she caught his gaze. "I'm sorry. I was just . . . I'll save it for when you can eat it."

Skokes nodded. "Sure . . . not likely though." Bile still stung his throat.

"Are you all right?" She touched his arm with her human hand.

Skokes waved her off, a bit disturbed by her snatching up what he'd spat out. "I will be." He stood back up straight. "They just brought our food. We should have a few hours before They come for you again—give me a hand."

Bree put his arm over her shoulder, but he drew a sharp breath as the points of her transplanted scales dug into the muscle of his arm. With difficulty, he limped over to the grate in the ceiling. "I might be able to get through a few more bars in that time."

Bree pulled him back, her face glowing blue as she stood under the brightest part of the bulb's light. "I don't want you to go," she whispered.

"I'm almost through—if I get through fast enough, I'll be able to come back and get you . . ." he swallowed and his voice broke. He waited before continuing. "Before They do."

"Really?" She cradled his head to her neck.

"Really," he said into the now grainy, salty skin of her neck. "I want you out of here before They touch another hair on your head . . . so. . . ." He waited for her to give him a leg up. She finally nodded and cupped her claw and hand for him to step into. Skokes jumped up, groaning at the pain in his mangled leg and the stiffness in his muscles. Exhausted beyond belief, he half dropped, half fell back into the cell. But Bree got her shoulders under his legs the next time, and pushed him up to the bars. Grabbing the edge of the air vent, he seized the grate and pushed it aside. He swung his legs up but couldn't bring them as close into his body as he should have, and yelped when they hit the side of the opening.

Finally, he was up inside the passageway of the air vent. He looked back down at Bree, who mustered up a smile, touched her clawed arm to her forehead, and waved with her human hand.

"I'll come back for you," he said quietly, smiling, reaching his arm down into the room to her.

She stretched her human arm up as far as she could, standing on tiptoe, but their fingers just missed connecting. "John?"

"I promise."

She nodded and he pulled himself back into the passageway. *Lop-fi-eets-chay. Let us hunt.* Putting the dagger between his teeth, he crawled along backwards until he reached an intersection where there was another pyramid grid, but the cell below was unoccupied. However, there was enough room here for him to turn around and continue the rest of the way crawling forward. Halfway to the next grate, he felt a thick, slippery goo coating his hands. Grimacing, he held his fingers up to the light coming from the cell. Dark liquid dripped off his hand. He looked to his left. The creature he'd killed the last time had no head except for row upon row of serrated teeth and a mass of white eyes. Skokes poked around the teeth and touched a body covered with scaly spikes and the claws of a centipede.

"NO! NO! JOHN!"

Skokes's fingers caught on the spikes of the dead creature and tore them open to the bone. Bree's screams pierced the dank air of the passageway. "Bree!" He shouted louder and louder as he crawled faster and faster toward her screams. "Lop-fi-eets-chay, You bastards, let us hunt!"

The clicking of stones underwater drove like sharp metal through Skokes's eardrums into his skull. *I'm drowning, my head's going to burst.* Gasping, he tried to pop his ears against the pressure that filled his head, but it only grew worse, to the point where his heart pounded louder and slower against the inside of his head. He yanked himself along, groaning against the strain, dragging his bandaged leg.

"John! Help me!" Bree's scream turned into a guttural shriek. The clacking and clicking of stones matched the sluggish pounding in his skull. Skokes bit down on the dagger, forcing the words out through gritted teeth. "I'm coming, I'm coming, hang on—"

He reached the next pyramid grate. Dripping with sweat, Skokes cautiously took the dagger from his teeth and peered down into another humid cave cell, this one brightly lit. Directly below him lay a brownish-black metallic slab. They splayed Bree out on the slab. One of Them shoved her face to one side and pinned it down with a giant claw. Some kind of equipment—shiny black, covered with long luminescent green spines—surrounded her head. A second claw pulled on one of the spines that bent and twisted hungrily as It directed it toward her face.

"No! Al-La-Pa-Taw!! Don't take her!" Seizing the dagger, Skokes reached through the grate and jabbed it deep into the back of the giant creature. "Yo-He Wah!!!!" he screamed, invoking the god whose name he'd been warned never to say aloud.

Bree's head turned as he did and her eyes widened in recognition, but the other creature cracked her head back against the slab, dazing her, and yanked at one of the snaky green needles. The doctor reached up in one detached movement, grabbed Skokes's arm and tugged. Skokes screamed as his shoulder dislocated again. Still holding Skokes's arm, the doctor yanked the dagger out of the other creature's back and pressed it into Skokes's wrist, severing his hand from his body. The pressure in Skokes's head burst and he passed out.

"John?"

Skokes's eyes fluttered open. He tried to speak, but his throat was ripped raw. Blood soured his mouth. "Bree?" he finally managed to whisper.

Her head was cocked all the way into a 180-degree angle now, showing him only a side profile. Her eye rolled down, gazing fixedly at him. She wiped his forehead with a rag ripped from the flight suit, dipping it now and then into the water pool next to them. He gasped as some of the water dripped down his throat, scalding the raw skin with its coolness. A single tear ran out of Bree's eye and down her cheek, splashing and stinging Skokes's eye. "They've cut off your hand," she said quietly.

Skokes blinked away Bree's tear and struggled to bring his arm to his face, but she held it down beside him. "No," he groaned.

"Don't move. . . . I didn't think the bleeding was going to stop. I thought I was going to lose you, you've been unconscious for so long. . . ."

Skokes stared at her and reached up with the arm she wasn't holding down. "He-a-maw. Come here." He turned her head to face him.

The other half of her face was elongated and darkened, the color of a cancerous melanoma. A jowl had swollen under her once gaunt cheek. Something was stuffed where her eye used to be. Now a sulfur-yellow eyeball slit down the middle yawned into a black maw gliding lazily along the top of the swollen jowl. Her lips stretched back over long, sharp triangular teeth. She turned away to face him with her human side again. "Don't."

"I'm sorry," he whispered.

"It's not your fault." She gurgled a bit as she spoke and drooled on him. But the drops that fell on his face had a strong, familiar salty taste. Skokes flinched as if he'd been bitten.

Why is this taste familiar? He stared up at the air vent, now sealed by black rock. *Why am I so frightened? What have I done wrong?* Tears filled his eyes. "I'm going to break my promise," he said. She released his other arm. He raised it slowly and looked at the bandaged stump for a long time. Finally putting it back down at his side, he closed his eyes. Then he opened them and looked into her waiting steady gaze. "We won't be getting out."

Bree swallowed and tried to smile, but it came out more like a grimace. "I know," she said softly.

"Not now." He took a deep breath and felt the old twinge in his side from his father's kick. He closed his eyes again and saw the shiny obsidian rocks of his mother's grave glittering in the sunlight of the canyon of his old home. "We have to end it ourselves. I can do it so you won't feel anything, I promise. Before They come back. We'll do it now."

Bree nodded and lowered her head.

"The greatest warrior." He sat up with a groan and moved behind her, wrapping his maimed arm around her throat in a chokehold. With his good hand he gripped her head, poised to break her neck.

"Close your eyes," he said quietly. When he closed his own, he saw the crocodile crawl up on the dried embankment. Tears streamed down his face. "Bree, I want you to know—" The words choked in his throat.

"I know," she whispered and gently placed her claw over his maimed arm. He nodded and leaned his head against her grotesque jaw. They sat that way almost forever.

"I can't—"

"It's all right, John." Bree swallowed hard and sucked in drool through her gaping jaws. "I had hope for a while. You gave me that, it was a gift. . . ." Her head turned side to side slowly. "But that's gone now." She paused, her mouth bubbling as she breathed. "Hope for us, hope for humanity. . . . I just don't feel it anymore. So I want it to end now. Che-ho-shar. Chi-ho-ches-chee."

You are lost, I am lost. She does know. She is the greatest warrior. Skokes heard the clicking of stones underwater and he moved his mouth close to her remaining human ear and whispered, "Bree, you're right. You are lost. I am lost. But have hope . . . not for us, but for Earth. . . ."

Bree grew absolutely still. The heat squeezed in on them. Skokes had to swallow to reduce the pressure in his ears. He couldn't tell how loudly he was speaking now so he leaned right into Bree's ear. "They've held back a huge force of our best fighters on the far side of the sun. . . . Only a handful of people know it exists. We've led Them to believe we were on the brink of collapse, but thirty days from the day I was captured, they're going to strike *Their homeworld*. It'll be enough to turn the tide, Bree. In the end," he squeezed her neck instinctively, "we'll have won."

Bree nodded. Another tear rolled down her human cheek. Skokes kissed it away and tasted brackish water and the too familiar pungent, salt tang. "Thank you for telling me, John."

Crocodile tears. But there's no word for crocodile. Skokes jumped and flexed his muscles, finally ready. "I wanted you to know. . . . Forgive me." He tightened his arm around her neck, and placed the heel of his hand against the back of her head.

The cell doors flew open and the jailer rushed into the room. Skokes tried to snap her neck, but Bree's own hand yanked his off of her. Simultaneously, the jailer struck him and sent him flying across the room. He landed with his remaining hand in the acid pool. Screaming, Skokes jerked his hand out of the pool and half groped, half hobbled to the doorway where the jailer was leading Bree out by the hand. "Take me, instead . . ." he demanded, crying, then begging, "don't change her . . . leave her a hoke-tee-ti-mi-nit-ti-tee, leave her a young woman. Please don't change her anymore!"

Both the jailer and Bree stopped and turned to face him. Although the jailer was easily twice her height, It still seemed dwarfed by her huge jaws. *Tristan. Tumult, din.* Her reptilian side peered at him, her tongue quivering against her saw-like teeth. "You don't understand, John. They're not changing me." Her mouth gaped, and Skokes saw the milky fluid pooling in her triangular jaws. *Our children. Our human children.*

There's no word for crocodile, came his dream mother's voice. *It wasn't "use this" she was saying, it was Il-it. Death.*

"They're changing me back."

No more four corners. Hundreds of stones clicked together like rain as she slurped her mouth closed.

Osceola. Eight. Ate.

The Bree Thing slid the door closed.

Skokes found the crystal dagger, and drew it across his cheek, smearing the blood all over one half of his face. But the tears kept washing it away. "I have done nothing to be ashamed of. It is for those to feel shame who have entrapped me." He covered his neck with blood, closed his eyes, and bowed his head. Opening his eyes, he saw a drop of semen by his knees. He touched the tip of the dagger to it. "We never surrendered, we were never conquered," he whispered and cut his throat.

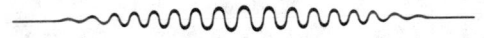

PHOEBE REEVES *teaches Composition and Expository Writing at the University of San Francisco and the City College of San Francisco, at all levels from developmental to advanced. Her composition textbook,* What's the Big Idea?: Discovering Writing Through Reading and Thinking, *will be published by Prentice Hall in August of 1997. Her short story,* "Eyes Like Stars," *was published in* Midnight Zoo, *and she also adapted it into a radio play, which aired nationally on Shoestring Radio Theater.*

Barkley, Claridge, and Wells spent three entirely reasonable months on Mars, collecting geological samples and getting along perfectly well. But on their last night on the planet, their last walk on the surface, they found an alien artifact. Despite the explosion it caused, and the problems they had getting it back to their spaceship, they had no way of knowing that taking it onboard would irrevocably change their voyage home.

The Voyage Home

Adaptation by Diane Duane
Original Screenplay by Grant Rosenberg

It was something of an unscheduled jaunt, that final walk outside the Mars 3 spacecraft. The EVA had not been cleared with ASA, but the three astronauts on the probe had been allowed a certain amount of leeway, a certain discretion in scheduling extra walks when they could make an adequate case to Mission Control. . . . At least, when the proposed walk was not too greedy of time or resources.

When they proposed it, Megan in Mission Control simply shrugged and said, "Just log your times in and out, and have fun. . . ." Had she pressed the point, Barkley's excuse would have been that he really needed to do a walk round his craft. Some pilot-habits died particularly hard. He had never been able to take off with any kind of comfort without a long, slow walk around to see that the wings were still fastened on tight and that the tail didn't show signs of falling off abruptly. That tendency had saved his life, once or twice: a hairline crack spotted here, a fastening not quite fastened there. . . .

Today, he also would have had the excuse that they needed to check just one more time to make sure that all the equipment was in: even though Wells had taken his usual care with the checklists. The cost of getting all this equipment to Mars and home was on his mind. Barkley knew how the taxpayers hated to lose even one hundred-thousand-dollar torque wrench, and how certain Congressmen with nothing better to do could make an issue of such a piece of mislaid equipment.

It was a little disappointing, in retrospect, that Megan hadn't even pursued the issue, when he was so ready for her. *Oh well,* he thought. She'd find something else to tease him about, and he'd return the compliment, and turn it into yet another way to ask her for a date. It was part of the old dance, and he never got tired of it.

The others had nodded understandingly as he'd outlined his agenda to them. They'd known perfectly well—and who better?—the real agenda for the extra walk. Barkley wanted to get out on that surface just one more time. One more walk out in that howling red desert. . . . And the others wanted that walk as badly as he did.

So they took it, ambling off in the direction of a small group of hills with a system of crevasses on the outside. They had barely had a chance to investigate those hills toward the end of the mission, having been much too busy with sites in other directions that ASA had targeted for their investigation long before they took off. With all the scheduled sites now covered, they had a little time to spare.

Barkley privately thought it was a hell of a time for Wells to indulge his fondness for spelunking. Himself, he preferred the open desert: bleak and cold as it was, even now in the Martian summer. That screaming wind came howling across, pushing the ever-present red dust across at you: drinking the heat away from your space suit as fast as the heaters could replace it.

He had no quibble with the weather, really: it had been an unseasonably warm 3 degrees Fahrenheit for almost a week and a half now. *Typical,* he thought, *that the best weather of the vacation comes when you have to leave. . . .*

The others weren't completely sympathetic to his view of the landscape. They didn't stand out there quite as often or as long as he did, gazing across at the endless foreshortened rocky flatness—that horizon that seemed three times closer than it should—to the purple-black sky as it came down to meet the ramparts of the horizon like a painted backdrop, with the pallid little dime-store sun hung in it like a bare hundred-watt bulb, and giving about as much heat. The light was indescribable, especially toward sunset, when the ground itself almost seemed to glow from inside, like a lava light: a glow he had seen lingering deep in mountains in the Dolomites, in as bitter a wind, and with a sky almost the same color. There was a lowering, threatening, uncaring beauty about it all: until night fell, when (except for the stars) everything was as dark as the inside of a cat.

He thought about the outsides of cats as they walked: his own tiger tabby purring in his lap when he got home. *Howler,* he thought, *you wouldn't think much of this place even at its warmest. No birds to catch, and the sun could be out all day, but you wouldn't get any warmer.* And he shivered a little. Warmth, the beach, a sun that gave heat. *Home....*

He put the thought aside for the moment, looking ahead as they walked. It was getting dark: not that the nighttime bothered them much now when they were exploring. For the first couple of weeks they had been cautious, very cautious indeed, after nightfall. Each of them had caught himself looking over his shoulder when the darkness came down, and hurrying "home": as if Mars had burglars who might break in after dark and steal their stereos. After a week or so, though, they had grown more cavalier about it . . . though not entirely casual.

Now the lights of the spotlamps they were carrying made jagged circles on the rough stone of the cave walls. Going carefully, watching their step in the outer reaches of the cave where the walls were close together, they found some stalagmites poking up from the floor: it was easy to trip, and they went slowly. "Come on," Wells said, "it opens out up here."

The atmosphere was thin, but not so thin that it couldn't carry a little bit of sound; inside an enclosed space like this, the muted, muffled echo was very strange. You heard it more through your suit than through the air, or so it seemed.

Barkley looked around. Cold gray stone, dust. . . . He thought of his sister-in-law, a tidy-minded woman: he could just hear what she would say about all this dust. He was glad she never saw his housekeeping inside the spacecraft. Dust got in no matter what you tried to do about it, and even the (apparently) hundred-thousand-dollar specially designed vacuum cleaner seemed to do little more than stir the dust around, rather than pick it up. Or if it did pick it up, more always got in. . . .

He scuffed briefly at the dust with his toe, and watched it kick up, float only very briefly, and settle down again over his spacesuit boot.

"Oh, my God," Al Wells said suddenly. "Over here. Look. . . ."

The tone of his voice made Barkley look up immediately. You didn't get that kind of urgency with Al as a rule. He and Pete teased Al sometimes about being a throwback to the older days of astronauting, born out of his time: the kind who would have taken having electrified hypodermic needles shoved through his hand without a second thought, as long as it got him into space. He would have sat there, grim, with a slight smile on his face—just enough to let you know that you were wasting your time if you thought you were going to get between him and the sky. Now, though, Barkley actually heard Al gulp. He went over and looked at where Al was shining the light from his spotlamp.

Then Barkley swallowed too.

"What've you got?"

"It looks like some kind of writing."

From behind, Claridge came along, very quietly, as usual for him, and looked over their shoulders. He was a big, dark, good-natured man, but now just a little of the good nature deserted him, and the breath went out of him in a huff of annoyance. "Unbelievable," he said.

Barkley felt the same way. They stared at the graceful, curving carvings in the wall. They were deeply incised: there was no question of them being accidentally or naturally formed. There was purpose in their grace.

"After three months of exploration," Barkley said, annoyed, "it *would* be only fitting to make a discovery like this on our last day."

"These are definitely man-made. I mean, some other kind of intelligent creature."

They all stood around the carvings, tense with annoyance. None of them had brought a camera: they had all been so sure there was nothing left to find, after four months of nothing more exciting than subsurface ice and endless rediscoveries of fossils of *E. coli arietis*. . . .

"Unbelievable."

"There *is* intelligent life out here."

"Or was. This looks like it's been here for a long time." Claridge brushed at the carvings with his glove.

"The people who buy into that 'face on Mars' thing are gonna eat this up," Wells said. As they stepped away from the carvings and shone their spots around, looking for more, Claridge favored him with one of those "oh-really" expressions in which he specialized. "If this writing is here," Wells said, "who's to say the face might not be real? Maybe it was left behind by an alien civilization as some kind of beacon...."

As they walked through the chamber, they found more carvings. "They seem to extend the entire length of the cave," Claridge said. "Oh, God, for a camera! We could be looking at the goddamn Rosetta Stone of Mars and not know it."

"Or at a recipe for Martian Swedish meatballs," said Wells grimly. "We can't just walk away from this. I'm going back for that camera." He turned, though not before shining his spot a little more deeply into the cave.

He froze where he stood. "Dear God. Barkley, Claridge!"

If the earlier call had been urgent, this one was almost strangled. They went to him, shone their lights alongside his.

On the floor before them, off to one side, nestled up against a wall, half-buried in fragments of stalactites, was a long cylinder or pod or something bluish—metal? Stone? It was almost spindle shaped, pointed at the ends.

"What do you make of that?"

"I have no idea."

They looked at the thing. Barkley looked at the others, filled with elation and even more annoyance, and something bordering on anger. *Why* does *it have to be the last day?* . . .

"What do you think it is?"

Al was looking at the thing now, sizing it up. "Don't know."

"Can we get it back to the ship?" Claridge said.

Wells looked at it, reached down, touched it with his glove . . . tried to find a handhold, then grunted with effort as he tried to lift it.

Wells straightened a little, shook his head. "It's too heavy. See if we can find an opening, somewhere to grab it. . . ."

Claridge leaned over to help him, and Barkley watched them, prepared to do the same. There was precious little room in the lower holds now—they had collected as much sample material as they could—but things could be rearranged somehow: a lot of sample stuff would wind up in their quarters, though, and someone was going to wind up with rocks in his bed . . . probably they all would. Still, for the sake of something like this. . . .

He leaned in, ran his hand down it, under it, wiggling his fingers and trying to find a place where he could brace himself, and then they could give it all a good heave together.

In the darkness, with only the relatively dim lamps for contrast, the burst of flame, like lightning, and of seemingly incandescent gas, was utterly blinding. The force of the eruption, or explosion, threw all three of them either into the nearby wall, or out into the central floor. Barkley had an impression, probably an optical artifact, of something like a twisting snake of light that ran up through the incandescent vapor. As he was thrown back, just as he had time to think, somewhat anticlimactically, *Uh oh*. . . .

Then the lights went out . . .

. . . leaving the feeling of something moving past him in the darkness.

Flickering light in the dusty darkness . . . apparently the lamp had been damaged by the explosion, or its subsequent impact against the floor or wall. Barkley blinked at the spotlight. He could see Wells's spacesuited shape, and not too far away, dimmer, Claridge's, moving weakly.

Wells was starting to sit up, holding his head like a man who's just realized he has a hangover, and how bad it is.

"Everyone OK?" Claridge said.

Wells finished struggling up, touched the outside link for his suit radio.

"What the hell happened?"

"We were unconscious almost an hour," said Barkley. "We've got just enough air left to make it back to the capsule."

Wells cursed. Claridge made a face, the sight of which almost made Barkley laugh, for this was as close as Claridge ever got to cursing: often enough, after some minor mishap when the other two let fly, he would look at them mildly and say, "If I use language like that every day, what will I have left to use when I hit myself with a hammer?" But now he made that annoyed face with a vengeance. "And we've already pushed our launch back as far as we can," he said. "If we don't lift off in four hours, we'll miss our window."

"Great," Barkley muttered. "We have the find of the ages, and we can't stick around long enough to document it properly. . . ." But there was nothing to be done about it. He thought, with some slight rue, that there were going to be questions about this when they got home. *What if you hadn't awakened when you did? X billion dollars lost on a missed launch window and three dead astronauts, blah, blah, blah. . . . Oh well,* Barkley thought. At least they were all alive and functioning.

Barkley stood, felt a little uncertainly for his balance—he was a little light-headed. That bright light had been astonishing: he could still see a faint afterburn image of it against the dark, a green phosphene glow. *Hope my retinas haven't been damaged. . . .*

They went back to the capsule-like object, and played their lights over it. It had an almost perfect circular hole in it now, but that was all. Some kind of malfunction, maybe. Likely enough: *God only knows how long the thing was lying here. . . .* Or some kind of reaction provoked by their touch, or just by their entry into the cave . . . even, for all they knew, by some change in barometric pressure. Barkley shook his head.

They all breathed out sadly, and then walked away. There was no time to come back. The next mission would have to handle that. All they could do was describe the writing, and the pod lying in the dust. . . .

They trudged back to the ship, and finished the last of the unscheduled tie-down tasks before they started the three-hour-long prelaunch checklist. And all the while they ran down the list, a little voice said in the back of Barkley's head, *Are you going to be able to accurately describe what you saw, three hours from now . . . ten hours from now? You've lost the greatest asset of the scientist: the freshness of the moment, the accuracy of immediate recall. . . .*

He sighed, went on with the list. There wasn't much else he could do: not much to record, either, except the size and shape of the thing, the color of the material it was made of, and the explosion, the snake of light—

—and something moving in the light—

Barkley blinked. *Artifact,* he thought. Just a memory of the phosphene, the burnt-in afterimage. Something about the way it moved reminded him, oddly, of the way Howler would move around in the dark at home, having come in from some business outside in the night: soft footfalls going by, quiet and intent. . . . Barkley sighed and shook his head. He would talk to the others about it: he doubted if he'd seen anything which would matter. . . .

Two hundred days later, the subject had been talked into the ground, and other pleasures had replaced the endless discussions of Martian spelunking and ancient Martian civilizations.

It was third down and ten to go. Two of them were on their feet, and shouting. The third was sitting and looking at the other two as if they were head cases.

The area was not exactly the image of the great American living room. If any motto summed up the living quarters of the Mars 3 astronauts, it was 'better living through electronics.' Wiring and grids and panels and controls—but then again, this place was built for function, not for comfort. Barkley had heard Wells mutter often enough that he knew dog pounds better furnished than this. Certainly there were times when the feeling of being in a cage with three other primates—and alpha-males at that—got stronger than usual. However, today was fortunately not one of those days.

Wells was sitting making notes on a pad, probably something for their pre-landing list. *Landing*, Barkley's heart said, and shivered inside him. Oceans, fresh air, something as desirable but inaccessible as Coca-Cola—he put all these aside for the moment. Wells was looking tolerantly at him and Claridge, whose whole attention was on the screen, and NU's performance.

". . . the NorthAm bowl hangs on this play," the announcer was shouting, which was unnecessary, since Barkley knew this too, and was shouting over him. "Defense, defense," Claridge was urging, and Barkley was shaking his head, yelling, "Intercept! Intercept!" Figures stirred on the screen, moved, maybe half a million miles away.

"Everyone in the country, including the Mars 3 astronauts, who are on their way home and watching this telecast, are wondering if Northwestern can pull it off again."

"Hey, nice plug," Wells said mildly. The others ignored him.

"Come on, put it in the end zone, NU."

"Hold them, boys! Hold 'em, hold 'em—"

It was wonderful to be close enough again to earth, where you could root for a football team and know you weren't too late: the game wasn't already won or lost five minutes ago, or half an hour ago. Maybe it was silly that this should matter. Even for a game delayed by tape rather than by lightspeed, your emotions were no less valid. But that feeling of immediacy, of shouting encouragement and having it responded to right *now*, that was something you could learn to miss.

Figures moved on the screen. A flurry of motion—and Barkley jumped from the bed, yelling "Interception! *Yes!*"

"Interception," groaned Claridge, and covered his face with his hands in an I-don't-believe-this gesture.

"He's going . . . going. . . . Northwestern scores as time runs out!" yelled the announcer. "What a finish to NorthAm Bowl 12!"

Claridge sat down, looking with resignation at the screen. Wells glanced at this moment of pathos, and went back to his notes.

Barkley, for his own part, was pacing back and forth with great glee. "Ever since Northwestern left the Big 10 they've kicked butt. Who'd have thought it!"

"Wait until next year," said Claridge desperately.

"Maybe, but in the meantime, you owe me a hundred bucks. Payable when we get home."

Claridge gave him a look containing an even heavier dose of resignation. "Just don't tell Jenny. She'll kill me."

"You kidding? Jenny loves me. She'll be happy to hear that you contributed to my retirement fund."

Wells got up with the look of a man who was relieved to be able to finally turn off the football game. "All right, guys, it's time. Let's see if Houston's home."

He made an adjustment to the controls: the screen flickered. "Houston. This is Mars 3. Come in."

Nothing: the screen made snow. They had overrun the scheduled check-in time by about ten minutes, as Barkley knew; and Wells, ever the stickler for doing things by the book, had started to chafe gently but visibly when the game ran into overtime.

"Houston. This is Mars 3. Come in. . . ."

The screen flickered. Megan's face appeared on screen, in front of her own computer, and with one of the light StarSet talk-and-listen headsets on. She was in her late 20s, a young woman handsome rather than pretty: dark shoulder-length hair, a businesslike expression, and wearing a softer version of the eternal flight controllers' uniform; shirt, tie, and suspenders—*why do they always wear suspenders?* The only thing different about Megan was that she did not have the otherwise universal flight controllers' slight Texas drawl. That made her stand out. So many of them had trained in the same facility, or with teachers who themselves had trained in that facility, that everywhere you went, from Quito to West Africa, you still heard that civilized drawl.

Megan, though, somehow sounded like she had just escaped from Bryn Mawr or some other select Ivy League establishment. She looked more like a broker or an investment banker than someone with a doctorate in rocket physics. "This is Houston, Mars 3. We're reading you loud and clear. How is everyone feeling today?"

"You try waking up with these jokers every day for a year and a half," Wells said, very dry, "and see how *you* feel."

Barkley smiled at Wells's traditional anti-jock act. It surfaced now and then: he and Claridge had learned to laugh it off quite early in the flight, and they got plenty of further practice each week when the routine download of *The NFL This Week* arrived.

"Are you kidding?" Barkley said. "We're three days from home, and my alma mater kicked UVa's asses all over the field. Life is perfect."

Megan gave him what Claridge had once described to Barkley as "an old-fashioned look." "We're on an open channel here, Mr. Barkley. Please restrict your language."

"Sorry. 'Stomped' their asses. Is that better?"

She laughed a little. "I believe I speak for all of ASA when I say we will be very happy to have you back on terra firma."

"I'll make you a deal. One date, and I promise to be a good boy."

She eyed him in a noncommittal manner and shook her head gently: her expression was indulgent. "I'm afraid that wouldn't wash with my husband."

Barkley *tsk*ed in a disappointed way. Claridge leaned closer to the monitor and said, "Houston, this is Claridge. How're my wife and kids?"

Megan smiled. "Fine, and looking forward to seeing you, Doctor."

"Tell them I miss them. . . ."

"'And I love them very much,'" Wells and Barkley said in a heartfelt but very bored chorus, backup to Claridge's solo. Amused, Barkley said, "Come on, Pete. I think by now they know how much you love them."

"You wouldn't understand," Claridge said, leaning back in his chair and sighing. "You don't have a family."

"Three ex-wives don't count?" Barkley said, attempting to at least sound injured.

Megan chuckled. "We're ready for your status report, Commander Wells," she said.

Wells said, "Well, in the last twenty-four hours we've—"

The crash and thunder that went through the ship knocked them all to the floor. Lights dimmed; the screen flickered and lost its image. There was a brief, heartfelt groan from the structure of the ship; something being strained, strained—and reluctantly not giving way. Suddenly, all that dust which had gotten in and supposedly been vacuumed up was in the air again, shaken out from wherever it had been hiding; and the alarms began shrieking, high, low, and in between.

Wells reached up, hit a couple of controls, and said, "Everyone OK?"

They muttered acknowledgment, though it was questionable whether anyone could claim to be all right when that racket was going on.

"OK, move to the bridge," Wells shouted, swarming up the ladder to the command deck. "I want the details now!"

"Best guess," Barkley said, going hurriedly after Claridge, "something hit us! . . ."

Upstairs, they still had light and power, but the power was flickering. Things looked very unsteady; readings were fluctuating wildly as the power came and went.

Wells was already at his command console. "I have telemetry," he said. "Give me some numbers. . . ."

Barkley hit the controls to bring the telemetry feed up live. "Probably a micro-meteorite," he muttered. But no sooner had he touched the telemetry panel than it spat fat sparks at him, and a jolt grabbed hold of him and threw him right down on the floor. Fire erupted inside the console.

Stars exploded in his head as he went down; he had hit his right temple on something, heaven knew what. Stunned, Barkley could only lie there for a moment and moan. Overhead, he heard the shout, "Get that fire!"

He was struggling to get to his feet when Claridge ran past him with a fire extinguisher and played it over the burning console. Barkley managed to grab hold of the seat of his own station, pulled himself up, and sat in it. He began tapping at the keyboard, ignoring for the moment the blood he could feel trickling down his forehead. The noise of the alarms and shouts started filling the whole world. "We're off course!" Wells yelled. "Primary guidance system down—"

Barkley turned his head—almost threw up with the pain of doing so—and yelled at Wells, "We're down to 35,000 mph, off course 20.01 degrees port. Get ready to manually fire the boosters."

Wells nodded, hammering on his keyboard. "Give me the numbers."

Barkley stared at his screen, but none of the numbers made any sense. In fact, he couldn't understand what he was looking at at all. He closed his eyes, shook his head, and stared again.

"Barkley, the numbers!"

Yes, the numbers, Barkley thought; and suddenly they shook down and once more made sense. "OK," he said, "give us a twelve-second burn on number three booster."

The boosters fired. Over Wells's panel and his own, a screen showed a representation of the ship's course status, like a view down a long grid-marked hallway, narrowing to a vanishing point at infinity. They were well off to one side of the hallway, threatening to drift right out of it.

"Get ready for a four-second burn on number two," Barkley shouted. But another panel flew open, spitting sparks. Claridge was on it, spraying it with the fire extinguisher. He headed past the ladder toward another smoking panel. Barkley saw him glance at something on the ladder, and then move on, spraying the extinguisher again.

Wells was still working at his keyboard, wrestling with his joystick. Barkley was finding it hard to concentrate; the noise in the ship fought with the pain in his head, and every now and then the swimming feeling descended on him, and he found himself staring at a screen filled with gibberish, at numbers which no longer made any kind of sense.

"Ed, you all right?"

He was decidedly not all right, but this was not the time to be admitting that to anyone, lest he himself become convinced of it. "Booster number two . . ." he said to Wells, ". . . now."

Slowly, slowly, the ship began to come back into trim: the virtual "hallway" was square once more, and they appeared to be moving smoothly down it.

"Five seconds," Barkley said. "Four. Three. . . ."

Wells counted the burn down with him, and stopped it right on the tick.

Sudden silence. The sound of a ship no longer groaning . . .

. . . for the moment.

Wells leaned back in his chair, breathed in and out once, as if letting all the tension out of his lungs in one go. "Good job, guys."

Claridge put the fire extinguisher away, paused by Barkley. "Let me get a look at your head," he said.

Barkley was unwilling to let himself be ministered to at the moment: that would mean relaxing, and if he did that, he thought he might pass right out when he was most needed. "It can wait," he said, and went back to milking what little telemetry he could out of his station. Things were improving slightly: at least some of the readout systems were now answering as their power source stabilized.

"Status report," said Wells, for all the world as if Barkley had not taken a nasty crack on the head and was not now nursing what was probably a mild concussion.

That's what I need from you, Barkley thought. *Support. Just be the way you are. . . .* He peered at his screen. "Good news and bad news," he said, as Claridge looked over his shoulder. "Hull integrity seems to have held."

Claridge blinked. "What's the bad news?"

"Communications are out, one power cell down, and our external oxygen tank is reading zero pressure."

Wells looked at him with some concern. "We've lost *half our oxygen?*"

Barkley started to nod, then thought better of it. "The impact must've caused the tank to leak."

Claridge noticed his pained motion and started toward the medical pull-down shelf off to one side while Barkley sat back in his chair and just stared at the screen for a moment, not wanting to have to deal with the uncomfortable numbers just yet. His eyes drifted down to a spot just beneath the screen, where a photo was taped, a picture of the three of them taken out at the beach near his home before they had left for the long pre-flight preparation period. Claridge with his dark, kind face; Wells, a little narrow-faced and waspish-looking, as usual, but wearing a smile over it all; and Barkley himself, big and blunt-faced and ironic-looking—he had never been able to smile for the camera without looking like an idiot, so he had given up trying some years back, and at least now his ironic expression looked presentable, and occasionally warm.

Half our oxygen, Barkley thought, looking at the image of his friends' faces. He could not think of two people he less wanted to have to play "lifeboat" with. But unless they came up with some options fast, it was going to come to that...

No, he said to the Universe. *I'm not playing. All of us get out of this... or none.*

He looked up and noticed that Claridge had stopped by the spot he had passed earlier, the post of the ladder down to the crew quarters and the service module. He stared at the post.

Wondering what his problem was, Wells got up to have a look.

After a moment, he said, "What is that?"

Curiosity was getting the better of Barkley; he got up too, came over to see what they were staring at.

"Don't touch it," said Claridge.

Barkley had no desire to.

A glob of something strange was stuck to the pole of the ladder. It was partly a sort of honey or amber color, but cloudy, and partly a sickly kind of green. It reminded Barkley entirely too much of something that had once come out of an infected finger he'd had as a child, when the swelling at the end of the finger was lanced. The memory was a little too much for his stomach, and he had to swallow and control himself before he trusted himself to say, "What is it?"

Claridge shook his head. "I have no idea."

He went off to get a Petri dish and an Xacto knife. With great care he used the knife to scrape off the glob into the dish: then he went off to the non-electron microscope.

In just a few minutes, he had a sample of the stuff on a slide and was studying it, while the others watched him curiously. After a moment he looked up over his shoulder and said, "You'd better take a look at this."

Wells peered through the binocular eyepieces. Claridge watched him look, and then Wells pushed away. "What is it?"

"I've never seen anything like it."

"It's probably some of that gel they use in the insulation," Barkley said. "It must've fallen from the ceiling panels when we got hit."

"But there's no trace of it on the ceiling," said Wells.

Claridge shook his head. "This is not insulating gel. It's living matter. And it's multiplying and changing form faster than I've ever seen any organism change."

"Which means?"

"I've seen just about every kind of microorganism on earth. And what I'm trying to tell you—is that this isn't one of them."

Barkley sat down to look at the stuff. Through the eyepieces, even on very low power, he could clearly differentiate two kinds of structures—long threadlike ones, very mobile, and thicker globules—all very active, as lively as the row-row-row-your-boat cilia of a paramecium. As they writhed and squirmed under the lens, there was an unnerving feeling of purpose about them.

He sat up straight, rubbing his head a little: the strain of looking through the eyepieces was troubling his throbbing head. "You're saying this is some kind of alien life form?" said Wells.

Barkley thought that that was entirely possible. "We must have picked up some microscopic organism from the planet and brought it on board with us."

Claridge nodded. "Maybe it came out of that thing in the cave—got into our suits while we were unconscious."

Wells shook his head. "I don't see how. All of our samples were hermetically sealed, and our tools and space suits were all decontaminated before we stowed them."

He was right there. Barkley thought a moment longer and added, "Plus, we've been on the return leg for over five months. Why would it just be showing up *now?* . . . Though you say it's multiplying really fast. Maybe it started with just one and multiplied to this point."

Claridge looked up, opening his mouth to say something, when there came a clunk and a hissing sound. Barkley rolled his eyes at the ceiling. He really wished he could just shout, *oh, now what?* The mission had run so smoothly until now. . . .

He and Wells made for the control systems readouts toward the back of the main cabin. Wells got to his screen first, looked at it, and swore. "There's a short in the passive thermal control unit. We've lost capsule rotation."

"Check the thermostat," Barkley said.

Claridge looked at another set of readouts and frowned. "Cabin temp is 78 and rising."

Wells got up, crossed to another console, and started typing at it with his usual demon speed—his answer to most problems. "We better get this crate rotating again fast or we'll fry."

"I'll go down and get on it," Barkley said, stripping off his outer jacket and heading for the ladder.

Claridge indicated the microscope. "Wait! What about this stuff?"

Wells waved one hand at the microscope, dividing his attention between Barkley and his own panel. "It'll have to wait. If I don't fix the rotation, we'll be too dead to care."

Barkley got ready to go down the ladder again, and once again felt that swimming feeling come over him. Wells looked up at him in concern.

"Are you all right?"

Barkley would have loved to say no.

Claridge looked over at Barkley and got up from the microscope. "Give me the tools. I'll go."

Barkley looked at him for a moment, hardly knowing him; and then the world reasserted itself. "I'm sure you could eventually fix it, Pete," he said, "but I'll fix it faster."

"It's 86 degrees in here and climbing," Wells said sharply, stripping off his jacket and chucking it over the back of the nearest seat. He sat down again and once more began working at the console. *Somebody go and fix the damn unit.*"

Barkley made his way down the ladder, feeling Claridge's worried eyes on him. "Hey," Claridge said from above, "be careful. There's a lot of very live stuff down in there."

This was an unnecessary warning, but Barkley smiled. "Don't worry," he said. "We are all going to walk out of this together. . . ."

"All for one, and one for all," said Claridge, and Wells joined in too, though looking a little wan. The Three Musketeers references were now such an old running joke among them that it had practically started to grow lichen. But now, somehow the oldest routines were the most reassuring.

Barkley came down into the hexagonal bay into which all the instrument clusters and storage areas were linked. He forgot momentarily that he was hurt, and as a result put his foot down harder than he should have on the bottom step. His skull went up in one big flare of pain, and he swore he could feel his brain rattling around inside it.

Barkley paused for a moment, thinking, trying to clear his vision. *Borderline concussion, almost certainly,* he thought. *Well, isn't this wonderful. At least I didn't lose consciousness.* He turned, rubbed blood away where he had touched his head, winced at the sight of it. Near him, something was dripping; never a good sound to hear in a spacecraft. *Coolant. Oh, hell.* . . . Barkley headed for the door of the engineering services module.

A tangle of wires hung down where one of the ceiling panels had given way. He ducked down and around the tangle, then slipped past it to the doorway leading to the engineering services wiring, and examined it for a moment. A punch of the button meant to bring it open produced an opening only about an inch wide; then the door groaned to a stop. "I'm at the unit," Barkley said into his headset.

Claridge's voice said in his earpiece, "How badly is it damaged?"

"I can't tell yet. The panel doors are wedged nearly shut. The walls must have gone out of alignment during that impact."

He could hear Claridge moving around upstairs, and commenting to Wells, "It just went from warm to hot."

There was a pause. "We're up to 94 degrees in here, Ed," said Wells.

Barkley snorted softly, and then wrote that down on a growing mental list of things not to do with an incipient concussion. "It's not exactly snowing down here, guys."

He leaned up against the door, put as much pressure on it as he could bear, and pushed sideways. The throbbing in his head became almost unbearable, but Al's words about being dead shortly were very much with him.

"Just my luck that the best made things on this ship are these damn door panels," Barkley said. He gathered his strength, pushed again, harder. With a groan, the door gave.

Barkley pushed it open far enough to slip in. He stood looking around for a moment. It was, as he had said, a mess. More wires hung down here, tangled, where there should have been tidy panels and neat gridwork, industrial shelving, and modules all in a row. Sparks spat as he slipped in and waved smoke away from his face. "Damn," he said softly.

In his earpiece, Claridge said, "Do you need a hand?"

"I'll let you know in a minute."

He boosted himself up on the shelf grid. Then he lay down on his back and used the grid to haul himself along into the confined space where he was going to have to operate.

"OK," he said, "I think I'm where I need to be."

In the earpiece, Wells's voice said, "How does the PTC unit look?"

"Barbecued," said Barkley. "I think I can fix it, but it's going to take a while. Shut off the secondary electric unit." The unit spat sparks at him as he spoke.

There was a pause, which he had partly expected.

"We'll burn up."

"I need it off to work on it or it'll fry me. Shut it down!" The PTC was spitting more sparks all the time, and he began to wonder whether it wasn't about to have a power surge that would fry him where he lay.

"That'll turn off what little air conditioning we're getting," said Claridge.

Barkley realized that if he let them just sit there discussing it, he could well be somewhere between rare and medium by the time they reached consensus. "I'm going in," he said grimly. "It better be off when I get to it."

Another pause. "It's going to be like an oven in here," Wells said.

"There's nothing we can do about it."

Silence. Then, "Secondary power has been terminated."

Barkley, within reach of the many-stranded cable that was causing most of the fireworks, sighed with relief. "OK. Al, you keep an eye on our levels and get ready to give me juice the second I've got this fixed."

"Okay, brother," said Wells.

Barkley looked at the cable, picking out the strands that first needed his attention. "Stand by and try to think cool," he said to the men above.

He tapped the cable in a gingerly manner, to see if it would spit again. It did nothing, which at least reassured him that it was not somehow shorting to one of the other systems nearby. All around him was the equally reassuring sound of machinery doing nothing.

All around him, it got hotter.

Up on the bridge, Wells and Claridge sat back in their chairs, trying not to move, and sweating hard. "Where are we?" Barkley asked from below.

Wells swallowed, blinked, looked up at the readout at his position, then glanced over at the image of Barkley, under the wire grid, like a creature in a cage. "Cabin temperature is 110 . . . and rising."

"You OK?" Claridge said.

Wells swallowed again. "We don't get this kind of heat up in Alaska. How can you stand it?" He laughed, but couldn't hide the slightly ragged edge to the laughter.

Claridge didn't move, simply sat with his eyes closed. "Growing up in North Carolina, you learn to adapt to all kinds of weather," he said.

Wells's breathing was getting more ragged. Claridge opened one eye, enough to glance over at him, and said quietly, "Everything will be fine as soon as Barkley gets the PTC back on line."

"He better be quick."

"We've come too far to fail now."

Wells squeezed his eyes shut, opened them again. His breaths were coming harder. He pushed up suddenly out of his chair, turned away from the consoles, and went over to the heavily reinforced glass doors that led to the EVA bay.

They were a bit of a luxury. Enough glass was set in them to actually let you see out through the little pane in the outer airlock, a tiny door into the depths of space—though the bright lighting inside the airlock reinforced the illusion that you were safely indoors, looking out at a little dark window no bigger than a TV set. Wells staggered up to the EVA bay door, leaned against it, pressed his face against the glass, and gazed out.

Claridge looked over his shoulder at Wells, a little concerned.

"Somewhere out there it's cold," Wells said softly.

Through the comm system, Barkley said, "Give me a reading!"

Claridge glanced again over his shoulder, expecting to see Wells on his way back to his post. But he was still standing with his face pressed against the glass. "Somewhere out there it's cold...."

Right out there, Claridge thought. What was it? ... ten, twenty degrees above absolute zero, this close to the sun? *A regular heat wave.* But no, the thought of heat was too oppressive. He shied away from it. In any case, Al Wells was not moving.

"Al," Claridge said, "get back into your chair. You need to monitor the telemetry."

But Wells was still standing there, gazing out toward the little square of darkness. "When this ship heats up another thirty degrees," he said softly, "we'll die. Eventually the capsule will crack, and our bodies will be swept out into infinity."

His voice was always a little thin; at the moment it sounded thinner than usual. "Al," Claridge said, "sit down and do your job. I want to make it to Earth."

"Even in death, we'll have no rest," Wells murmured. Slowly Claridge got up and went to stand near him.

"After our bodies explode into minute fragments, every molecule will float out there for all eternity...."

Claridge blinked. He had been extensively briefed about cabin fever; so had they all. But usually it was in the middle of long missions that the problem struck, during extended isolation—not toward the end, not when things were getting interesting, and certainly not in situations like this. He was not without sympathy for his friend, but they didn't have time for it right now.

He reached out, touched Al's shoulder—but Al spun swiftly away and knocked Claridge's hand away. Claridge looked at him, and it was a stranger's face suddenly: pale with more than the heat, the eyes a bit wild, the chest heaving, gasping—

Panic attack, Claridge thought. *Or for all I know, a full psychotic break. But those rarely happen without giving warning; and since when does Al panic—*

"Al, it's been a long trip," Claridge said. "It's perfectly understandable that you're feeling this way, but you have to hold on a little bit longer."

Wells blinked as Claridge spoke to him. Claridge smiled a little. "In a few days, we'll be at my cabin on the lake, reeling in those striped bass."

Wells looked at him again from a stranger's eye, tilted his head a little to one side, an exhausted gesture, and peculiar. "You don't have a cabin on the lake, do you?" And Wells laughed, a breath of edgy laughter.

Claridge stared. *What in the world is the matter with him?...*

"How is everything in there?"

There was a pause. Wells looked around as if he didn't know what to say. Claridge backed away from him, went to the screen, and sat down.

"Levels and telemetry are holding but it's getting hotter than hell. What's your status?"

Wells stepped over toward Claridge. Barkley said, "Making progress. And by the way, I've been to hell . . . my second marriage . . . and it's hotter than this."

Wells almost staggered back to his own seat and slumped into it. "Ed," he said, "how much longer?"

"A few minutes," Barkley said. "And do me a favor . . . have a cold beer waiting for me when I get back."

It was an old joke; ASA was dry, as the ESA astronauts who piloted *Buran III* and *Niña* had occasionally delighted in reminding ASA staff who went up with them on 'busman's holiday' missions.

Claridge chuckled, but the only sound from Wells was louder gasping, the rasp of the respirations becoming more alarming. Wells was sitting slumped in the chair, his eyes closed. His breathing was increasingly shallow, the seesaw "abdominal" breathing which sometimes means respiratory failure is near. Claridge got up, went past Wells and patted him on the shoulder. "Did you hear Ed? He'll have us back on line in a few minutes. Try to relax."

Wells's eyes followed him glassily as Claridge walked past him to the medication cabinet, pulled down its unfolding shelf, and looked over the syringes and medications racked there. He chose one, picked it up, and carefully tapped the air bubble out.

Behind him, Wells was gasping more loudly still. "The walls. . . . I can't . . . breathe. . . ."

"We're almost there," said Barkley's voice.

Claridge held up the syringe. "You see?" he said quietly.

With his back turned he did not see Wells's hand reach slowly out to the control for the PCT, and hit the button.

Downstairs, the sound of pumps powering up, the spit of sparks, were loud. Barkley yelled, at the top of his lungs, "Kill the power!"

On the screen, Claridge could see Barkley hanging on to the spitting, burning cable, keeping it away from him as best he could, but it was only a matter of time before it grounded itself on something—or on Barkley. "What the hell is going on?" he yelled again. *"Kill the damn power!"*

Claridge dropped the syringe and ran back over to Wells, throwing him out of his chair, and away from the control panel. Wells crashed to the floor, rolled, crouched where he had fallen. Claridge turned to the panel, while below, Barkley kept on shouting.

Claridge reached down and killed it. The pumps whined down to silence again.

"*You* might have a death wish," said Claridge, much more conversationally than he needed to, "but *I* plan on making it home." He hit the comm button. "Ed, are you all right?"

On the screen, he could see Barkley staring at his hand. The camera's definition wasn't good enough for Claridge to make out details, but Barkley's expression said a great deal. "My hand is toast," he said fairly nonchalantly, like someone giving a weather report, "my head hurts, and I have heat prostration, but other than that I feel great. *What happened up there?*"

Claridge looked over at Wells, who now lay on his back on the floor. He opened his mouth, closed it again, and then said carefully, "We had a temporary malfunction in the system. I think we've got it under control."

Barkley lay looking at his hand. "Well, I'll have something for you to play with in a while. We've got almost a textbook illustration of a third-degree burn here. Charring, cracking of the superficial tissue, the works."

Wells was rolling to his feet, nursing what might have been a cracked rib. Claridge threw a glance over at him, but couldn't feel terribly apologetic about it. The expression with which Wells favored him was an odd one, and unreadable. Exhaustion? Stupor? There was no deciphering it.

"What's the cabin status?" said Barkley.

Claridge glanced at the readout. "Temp is at 116," Claridge said, "and all other levels are red-lining from the heat."

Barkley looked at the cable again.

Claridge sat down at Wells's post; Wells was sitting with his back against the doors of the EVA bay, hunched, head down.

"Be ready go back on line the minute I give you the word, but not a second before."

"Roger," Claridge said.

Barkley took a long breath and then isolated the two wires which had been the cause of all the trouble, the white-and-red stranded pairs. He finished the job he had been in the middle of when the power came back on again: splicing each of them back together with its seared compatriot on the far side of the broken cable. His left hand was nearly useless to him at the moment, except inasmuch as it distracted him from his concussion. Later, he was sure he would pay the price for not being off somewhere cool, lying still, and recovering quietly; but there *was* nowhere cool, nor would there be until he finished his work. At least he was lying down. . . .

He used the palm of the burned hand to brace the cable against, and tried to concentrate on his work. The pain was beginning in earnest, now; for a short time, shock had protected him from the brunt of it, but you could only make shock last so long. Astonishing, though, how this blowtorch-like pain cleared his head.

He finished splicing the two wires together, wrapped them with insulating tape, and then let the cable go. He watched it swing briefly, and pulled away from it every part of himself that might possibly come into contact with it should the cable decide to start jumping around again.

"All right," he said. "Power up."

The soft hiss, growing louder; the sound of pumps coming up again . . . air, slowly beginning to flow. Cooler air. . . .

"We're back in business," Claridge said.

Barkley sighed. "I've got to reinsulate the wiring down here so we don't short again. I'll be up in a while."

Barkley looked at the cable: a half hour's work at least. He leaned back, first, and just breathed, and tried very hard not to weep at the pain in his hand.

"We're going to make it," Wells said, staggering to his feet again as the cool air began to breathe through the cabin.

"No thanks to *you*," muttered Claridge.

Wells threw him a look. "I don't know what happened," he said. "It must've been the heat." There was life in his eyes again, but also an expression eloquent of, not specifically betrayal . . . but that here was a man whose body had somehow not behaved the way he thought it was going to.

Claridge looked at him slowly. "Did you touch any of that stuff?"

Wells looked at him. "What stuff?"

"The organism, the white goo. Did you touch any of it? Did you ingest any of it?"

"No. Why?"

Claridge turned away, looking slightly exasperated. "Because you're not behaving like the Al Wells I know."

"Now that you mention it, *you're* not acting like the Pete Claridge I know."

"I'm not the one who went nuts back there."

"Oh, I see . . . so you think I swallowed some of that stuff and I'm infected with some kind of

Martian bug?" said Wells, sounding cranky, and laughed again, that slightly edgy laughter.

It did not sound like Al.

Claridge raised his eyebrows, got back up again, and went over to the lowered medical panel. He reached out for another syringe, pulled it out of its slot. It was a Vacutainer, an evacuated glass capsule with the needle for a blood sample attached. "I don't know what I think," Claridge said. "But I do know that the Al Wells I left earth with wouldn't have freaked like you just did."

"This is a joke, right?" Wells ambled over toward Claridge, who was busy with the Vacutainer. "Pete, you can't be serious. You've gotten incredibly paranoid all because of some strange bacteria."

"Maybe you're right," Claridge said as Wells sat back down again, wiping some of the sweat off his face. "But you can allay my suspicions with just a few drops of blood."

Wells looked at the syringe, then back up at Claridge. Claridge stood there, waiting.

"I think the heat's gotten to you," Wells said.

Claridge looked at him, thoughtfully. The expression in Claridge's eyes was definitely not the usual one.

"But," Wells said, "if it'll make you happy. . . ."

He rolled up his sleeve, held out his arm.

As Claridge reached out to take the arm, Wells reached forward suddenly and gripped Claridge's forearm with his own hand. Claridge looked confused for a moment, and stared at the arm. He felt . . . *something*. . . .

Wells looked up at him, and broke into a dreadful grin.

A little later, Wells stood with his back up against the central module in the bridge, hearing footsteps—Barkley coming up the ladder. At the top of the ladder they looked at each other. Wells's expression was odd: Barkley wondered if he looked as awful as he felt.

"Pete was feeling dizzy, so I sent him to lie down for a while. I think the heat got to him."

"How're the readings?"

"All our levels are back in the black. We're out of the woods."

"Not yet," Barkley said, sitting down at one of the nearby consoles and starting to work at it.

Wells looked at him with alarm. "What are you doing?"

"Shutting down all nonessential systems. We have to cut back our power usage by half."

"*Half?*"

"Also we'll need to ration our water intake to two ounces a day," Barkley said.

"But that's a quarter of what we need," said Wells. "Up here, water deprivation could be fatal."

"Cooling is at least as important as drinking. We don't have a choice," said Barkley, getting up from one console and moving along to another, making some adjustments there. "The next sixty hours or so will be tough, but we'll make it."

He finished keying in some instructions, then went over to the medical pull-down shelf and pulled out a roll of sterile gauze, unwrapping it. Slowly Barkley began to make a bandage for his burned hand, not wrapping it too tightly, for it would start oozing shortly. The ooze. . . . He wondered suddenly if Claridge had had any new thoughts about that.

"As soon as Pete comes back," Wells said, "you've got to get some rest."

Barkley stood there quietly, finishing the wrapping of his hand. After a moment he said to Wells, "You know, a lot of skeptics said I was pushing my luck, going up for a third time. Whichever one of you threw that switch almost proved those skeptics right."

Wells glanced away. "Why *did* you come, Ed?" he said after a moment. "I mean, I have to be honest, when I heard they passed you over for the number one chair, I figured you'd pass on the mission."

"My attitude didn't fit the mold of what a mission commander's should be. Yours did."

"But you couldn't pass up the chance to be the first man to walk on Mars."

Barkley shook his head, smiled slightly. "I figured I was only good for one more trip and this is the big one. I'm going to be able to write my own ticket when I get home. 'First man to step foot on Mars.'" The expression Wells gave him now was odd: he was shaking his head slightly. "It's got to be worth a few million in endorsements alone, not to mention the book deal and the lecture circuit. And the fact that we found evidence of life on the planet won't hurt either. It's like hitting the lottery."

"I'd like to think," said Wells, in a surprisingly flat voice, "that our discovery will have more value than to serve as a platform for your personal wealth and fame."

"Oh, of course it will. That's the beauty of it." Barkley finished wrapping the hand, and leaned down over Wells's console. "On the surface, we are the most altruistic people on the planet. We've sacrificed a year and a half of our lives on this mission and made the most important scientific breakthrough in space-travel history. In the meantime, we'll just happen to get filthy rich."

Wells's voice sounded a bit thinner than usual. "I think you're missing the larger picture. I mean, hell, we've seen that there is *life* out there."

"The scientific ramifications will take care of themselves. I worked my ass off for the ASA and NASA before them for twenty years; it's time for a little payback. . . ."

His eyes had been idly traveling over the familiar objects in front of him as he spoke: the EVA bay doors, Wells, the sweat-stains on Wells's clothes, the arm he was idly scratching. . . . His arm. Just under the sleeve was something that looked like a big cut, or a fissure, or a. . . . "What's that?" Barkley said.

Wells looked up with a slightly concerned expression. "Nothing."

"Roll up your sleeve!" said Barkley, more concerned than Wells was. It was an ugly-looking cut, infected from the looks of it. . . .

Wells looked up at Barkley, his eyes going wide. He suddenly got up out of his chair and took a couple of steps back. "I must have brushed up against something. . . ."

Barkley wasn't buying it. "Come on, Al," he said, "roll up your damn sleeve!"

Wells stared at him. Then, "It's not what you think. . . ." he said. He moved to roll his sleeve up.

. . . And revealed what Barkley had glimpsed: a long cut, a fissure down his arm, oozing the same awful pus-like ooze that Claridge had so carefully scraped off the pole of the ladder. Barkley stared at Wells, reached out for the communicator button on the panel, and hit it. "Claridge! Wake up!"

—But it was too late. Wells slowly looked up at him. It was an awful expression, of amusement, of a secret revealed . . . and dreadful intent.

Something lashed out and grabbed Barkley around his unburnt wrist. A tentacle, but with a bend halfway down its length, like an elbow. Barkley struggled to get loose: struggled, but in vain against—

What it was, he couldn't begin to say. It was lithe and green, with strange protuberances here and there. It was overtly upright, but not strictly bipedal. Whatever it was, it was caught in mid-change of form. Al's head still lingered horribly on top of it, atop what would have been shoulders in a man, but in this creature was just the place where two long, ragged, abnormally flexible limbs joined.

Al's head didn't last long, either. A shimmer, a movement like hot air rising, and Barkley was looking at a head more like that of an iguana—no, a parrot, that mean-looking beaky part—

Abruptly he hit on it: with the mobile eye, intelligent and nasty, and the overlapping plates ending in the sharp upper jaw, the creature was like a locust, a grasshopper, but inflated to obscene size. From the body of the creature, long spurs jutted, four of them, from shoulders and what might have been a waist. The arms were mottled like lizard skin, but chitinous too: insectile. That dreadful eye considered him as they struggled, and it tried to pull him close—

It was as if the creature was trying to do something to him, but wasn't able to, and halfway between outrage and horror, Barkley managed to rip his wrist out of the tentacle's grasp, and reeled back against the far wall. The creature shrieked in frustration, moved toward Barkley—

He shouted, rather hopelessly, "Claridge, get up!" He looked around him for a weapon, but there was nothing.

Then his eye fell on the fire extinguisher, and he looked at the insectile creature and jumped to a possibly useless conclusion. But it was better than nothing. *Extremes of temperature?* It didn't like heat very much. *Maybe cold?* . . .

It was worth a try, better than dodging around here waiting for the thing to throw its tentacles at him again, and maybe strangle him this time. Barkley feinted sideways. The creature feinted with him, but not fast enough. He let loose at it with the fire extinguisher.

The creature had a long tail, too, thrashing around like the tentacled arms, trying to reach him. But it couldn't reach him: it staggered back from the cold as if burnt. Barkley pushed his advantage, pushed the creature before him, playing the extinguisher all up and down it, but especially in its face. It screamed and flinched and backed away, screeching louder every time it took a blast of the cold in the face and eyes.

With his elbow, Barkley hit the door-open switch for the EVA bay. As the doors slid open, he blasted the creature full in the face again with the extinguisher. The thing that had been Al Wells staggered back, screaming. He gave it a good kick in the midsection to help it along, and a final shot of the fire extinguisher—then hit the door control once again.

The doors slid shut. The creature leaped toward them, but not soon enough. The pressure lock completed itself. On the far side of the doors the creature hammered and thrashed, and beat on the doors with those tentacles and that tail . . . to no avail.

Barkley stood there panting, looking at it.

From behind, Claridge's voice suddenly said, "What's going on?" Claridge had come up almost silently, as always, and now was looking past Barkley at the EVA bay, stupefied.

Through the glass, the Wells-thing was looking out again, beating on the glass, his face distorted with rage and fear.

"It's not Wells," Barkley said.

"Don't let him do this!" Wells screamed to Claridge. "He's crazy!"

"It's not Wells," Barkley said, grimly and with great certainty . . . and his hand was on the switch for the manual override of the outer doors. "It's not Wells—"

"He's crazy! Let me out of here!"

"Ed," Claridge said desperately, "don't do anything stupid—"

Barkley turned back to look through the glass at the shouting, terrified, raging, twisted face of Al Wells . . . and knew it wasn't Al.

"It's not Wells," he said again . . . and threw the switch.

The outer doors burst open. The Wells monster was sucked, flailing, out into the dark. He grabbed desperately, as he went, at the edges of the airlock.

It helped him not at all.

Inside the capsule, Claridge, horrified, pushed Barkley away from the door and pressed himself up against the glass. . . . Just in time to see the last few moments of Al Wells.

There are ways you can prolong your existence in vacuum, long enough to make your way back to a place of safety, a place where there's air. Close your eyes. Hold your breath. Your eardrums will rupture, but there's nothing that can be done about that, really. Minor capillaries will hemorrhage; exposed mucosa, in the nose particularly, will begin to freeze-dry. But these things only work if you have time to prepare yourself.

A man who is sucked screaming, eyes open, out into hard vacuum, with no warning, will not last even a fraction of the minute and a half that preparation will buy. The first great sneeze of blood, which is your lungs turning themselves inside out and exploding out of you, is just the beginning.

Claridge turned away from the door, and glared at Barkley.

Barkley collapsed into a chair, silent.

A little while later, Barkley stood by himself down in the crew quarters, gasping with reaction. He was not alone for long. Claridge came down the ladder behind him, watching him carefully.

"It was real," he said to Claridge, for about the hundredth time. "It was real. He had that goo oozing out of the cut on his arm, and that's when I realized it. Then the next thing I knew he was—" He turned, knowing how disjointed and crazy all this must sound: wanting to impress his friend with the fact that this was not something he was imagining or making up.

"Suddenly he transformed into this huge . . . thing. This thing, this alien *thing*." He almost wanted to laugh, then, but for pain, not pleasure. He had read and watched enough science fiction in his time to hear in the back of his mind the voice of a famous starship's doctor saying, a little scornfully, "Why does it always have to be a *thing?*" But the horror stripped him of the words; and every time he tried to find the words again, it occurred to him that trying to describe giant grasshoppers would probably not cut much ice with Claridge at this point.

But they had other problems. "God," he said, "where's Al? What did it do to the *real* Al Wells?" He lurched over to a seat and half fell into it, staggered by the thought. "Where is Al, Pete? *Where is Al?"*

Claridge looked at him with pity: the expression of a man who obviously thought that Barkley was losing it, or had lost it already. "You just ejected him into space. You killed him! Now listen to me...."

"You're not hearing me, Pete! *That wasn't him.*"

"OK, fine, *whatever....*" Claridge looked exasperated. "What's important now is that you let me help you...." He walked over to Barkley.

Barkley jumped up and started backing away from Claridge, steadily, as Claridge approached. "There's nothing wrong with me. It was *real.* It was obviously some kind of chameleon. More than a chameleon. It looked like him, knew everything there was to know about him. It's like it downloaded everything out of Wells's brain."

"Ed, you're not making any sense."

Barkley knew it. That was the worst part of all of this. He was a rational man: it was one of the things about himself that he had always known he could safely pride himself upon. Al might mention faces on

Mars, and Ed could kindly laugh out loud, but he could afford to be kind to his friend, at that point. Now that time seemed a hundred years ago. . . .

He did not believe in crop circles or UFOs or astrology or alien abductions . . . but aliens? . . . That had become another story entirely, in a matter of minutes. He was shaken to his core, terrified; and the worst thing about it was that he could not get Claridge to believe him, or to understand why he couldn't bear to have him near him.

"Let me look at your head . . ." Claridge said.

"Stay away from me!" Barkley yelled. Claridge looked bewildered.

But Barkley looked at him and said, "How do I know you're not one of them, too?"

The expression Claridge gave him was not quite pity, now. There was fear in it as well.

Barkley backed away, back to the ladder, and went up it almost in a rush. Claridge's mouth worked as he watched him go.

They did not speak much to one another for some time. The camaraderie which had made this trip bearable in its worst times, and a sheer pleasure in the best, was all gone. One part of it was forever gone now, amputated and aching. Another part of it sat across the cabin, looking out of that dark, friendly face, staring at Barkley with horror and concern. And Barkley . . .

... felt awful. His head still throbbed, his hand hurt worse than ever. ... He lifted the bottle of water, all that was left of a day's ration. There was one drop down at the bottom that he could not get to roll down the bottle's neck. He shook the bottle, scowled, dropped it clattering.

Across the console from him, Claridge looked up, reached out: held out a small bottle to him. There was still a little water in it.

"Take mine."

Barkley looked at him. "You can't tell me you're not thirsty."

"I'm parched, but you need to stay hydrated."

That thought had been occurring to him all too often. Having a third-degree burn of this size was the next best thing to having an open vein, in terms of fluid loss. Maybe a quarter of a pint an hour, maybe more. ...

"So do you. We still have over 36 hours left in this can."

"I can live without it for a while," Claridge said. "It's more important that you stay sharp. If something happened to you I'd never be able to get this ship back home by myself. It takes two of us to pilot it."

Barkley looked longingly at the water. Finally, "We'll share it later."

A flicker of light—the ozone smell of burning circuitry—sparks snapping. The smell of a short: and the alarms again. *Now, this is just unfair,* Barkley thought. *Everything was going so well.* ... "What was that?" he said.

"We lost another power cell. We're down to one."

Barkley consulted his own console. "Operating at one-third power and less oxygen."

"We can keep the oxygen levels in here steady if we seal off the rest of the ship."

Barkley glanced at the picture of the three of them that he had taped to the screen above his console. How often had they said, *The Three Musketeers? All for one. . . . All of us are getting home, or none of us are.* Now already only two of them were going to get home. Or maybe only one. Or none at all. . . .

But Pete was right. You couldn't run the ship with only one.

"Let's do it." He threw the switches to cut off the oxygen to the crew quarters and the other parts of the ship where they didn't need to venture. They would be a little island up here, now. They had no choice. . . .

"All available air will be restricted to the main cabin," Pete said, confirming, "and the service module."

"That's better."

Barkley sat back in the chair as the alarms stopped. Claridge's face worked as he leaned back.

Barkley got up, walked around to the other side of the console, and stood over Claridge. "Look, Pete . . ." he said sadly. "If you are Pete . . . I'm sorry for the way I'm acting. But if you saw what I saw, believe me, you'd be acting the same way."

Claridge looked up at him with great sorrow. "But I *didn't* see it, Ed. . . ."

And he just sat there, looking bewildered.

"I'm going to check the O² levels and power-cell levels in the service module," said Barkley, uncomfortably. Any excuse to get away from Claridge. "Make sure they jive with the readings we're getting up here."

He started down the ladder, one-handed.

He stepped downward with care, trying to avoid the jarring of that last step down onto the floor. Fatigue always made it harder.... He turned, looked around, checked the panels leading out from the service bay.

He wrinkled his nose, then. A smell—so many weird smells down here lately: burning insulation, ozone, chemicals.... This one, though, he couldn't identify....

He turned around, looking at the various doors. He'd been in all of them recently, except for the one where the EVA equipment was stored. Barkley hoped that door wasn't wedged, as the other one had been.

It opened easily enough, even though he had to do it one-handed. Barkley leaned in. The three spacesuits were in their brackets, their legs down flat in sitting position. Though one of them seemed to be sitting a little higher than was normal. And there was a faint....

Barkley reached down, snapped the suit's light on.

The suit was not empty. There was a body in it. The face paler than usual, eyes frozen open in an expression of deathly vagueness.

So he was less surprised than he might otherwise have been when, very quietly as always, Claridge came up behind him, and said, "We only had time to jettison one body."

Barkley hurriedly sidled away into the nearest open door, yet another service bay door. "Give me a chance to explain, Ed," said Claridge—or what had once been Claridge—but Barkley quickly slid the door closed, and locked it from inside.

And now what? he thought.

There was a period of silence. Then Claridge's voice spoke to him again, this time from the little loudspeaker pickup set in the ceiling. "Ed, I know this is a shock, but you've got to understand; the last thing I want to do is hurt you."

"You just plan to kill me and then duplicate me somehow...."

"I can only proliferate once every thirty-day cycle."

"'Proliferate'?" Barkley said, outraged. "Is that what you call what you do? That's an awfully polite word for sucking somebody's brains out, or whatever it is you do."

"Actually I introduce a spore into the body which maps the electrical impulses of the brain; then the spore leaves the body and replicates it. I can assure you that neither of your friends felt any pain."

"No pain, just *death*."

"Ed, relax," said Claridge's reasonable voice. "You have nothing to worry about. As I said, I only form one spore in every thirty-day cycle."

"Whew! I feel better," Barkeley said with no conviction at all in his tone. He turned away from the hidden camera pickup. It was unnerving to think that the thing living inside Claridge could see him, read his face, his movements . . . but he couldn't see it. Worse, he wasn't sure he *wanted* to see it. The honest human emotions and responses that had lived in that body were still there . . . but apparently no longer their owner's. The situation was horrible beyond description.

"Think, Ed. If I could proliferate through you, and if I wanted to, don't you think I would have already done it?"

Barkley let that go for the moment: he turned and faced the pickup squarely. "Who are you? Where are you from?"

"My race began billions of years ago on a planet many light years from your solar system. When our Sun died out, we had to find a new home."

"And you chose Mars?" That sounded a little stupid to Barkley.

Plainly, "Claridge" knew this too. He sounded a little rueful when he said, "When we settled there it matched the environment of our planet. However, several million years ago the atmospheric conditions changed on Mars, and my race died out. A small number of us were put into cryo-hibernation with the hopes that someday we would get an opportunity to begin again."

"In other words," Barkley said, annoyed by the bland phrasing, "you were left there for aeons as a trap waiting to spring on anyone unlucky enough to find you."

"And you will be glad you were the one who did. My culture is very advanced, and we have much to share with the people of Earth."

"You've already murdered two of my best friends. Is that what you call sharing?"

"I understand your reaction, but I wouldn't call it murder. The transformation of your Allen and Peter was unfortunate, but necessary for us to get off Mars. We could not live without taking their form and knowledge. Please believe me when I tell you that we are a peaceful species. Once I arrive on earth, I can promise there will be no more lives taken."

The voice was earnest enough . . . but Barkley was in no mood for this. Wells had been earnest, too.

And in the middle of the thought, another alarm went off.

Barkley jumped up, and the first thought that went through his head now was, *He's faking it.* Paranoia really was staggering, once it got hold of you . . . you started testing everything that happened: all trust was gone. . . .

He frowned at himself. "What is it?"

"I have a red indication on the cabin pressure monitor. There's a vapor stream coming from the starboard side, aft section."

"We're venting. . . . There is a breach in the integrity of the ship." It had to happen, sooner or later, with everything else that was going wrong. . . . And the grim humor of it struck him. "Guess I don't have to kill you. If we lose pressure, our lungs will explode instantly."

"You don't want to die up here." The voice was almost a little too persuasive. "Think of what is waiting for you back on Earth. The fame, the riches. . . ." But he would have traded them all, right now, for one sight of one genuine friend and fellow astronaut. But one of them was now a half-exploded, half-frozen mass of tissue and whatever that ooze was. And as for Claridge. . . . Barkley breathed in, breathed out, not knowing what to think.

"—you'll live out the rest of your life as a national hero. And, Ed, you can't deprive your people of the gifts that I bring. . . ."

He blinked. *What the—*

"Your mother died of cancer, did she not?"

He knew that. He *would* know that.

"I'll show your doctors how to cure cancer. Ed, I have the solutions to the problems your world has been pondering for years. You can go back and be the hero you always wanted to be. *But I don't know how to repair this ship alone.*"

He needed time to think. More than anything else, he needed time to think. And if he didn't do something, the ship itself, poor dumb thing, was going to take that option away from him. "I can't fix the ship either," he said, "one-handed."

"Then I think we should do it together."

For a long few breaths, Ed was silent. Then, "I'm coming up," he said.

He moved toward the door, unlocked it.

From the speaker came only silence: but it had an oddly satisfied quality . . . and there was a smile in it.

Ed came out into the bay, got his tools together. Shortly Claridge joined him. Barkley found himself trying hard not to stare, not to let his face reveal all the things he was thinking . . . and he was thinking so many different things, one after another, that it was a strain.

Barkley stared across the gridwork again, pointing for Claridge to see. "That valve right there," he said.

Under one of the protective grids was a pressure stopcock, with a long pressure-tight lead reaching away from it, wrapped in silver insulating bond. Barkley hunkered down, indicated it.

The thing passing for Claridge worked his way underneath to where the pressure fitting was venting gently. This internal vent was a small indicator of the problem with the larger vent outside. If they could shut this one down, they could shut down the outer one, too, and reroute the liquid nitrogen elsewhere into the system.

Painfully, Barkley made his way down amongst the cabling behind Claridge, favoring his hand. The hiss of the venting was loud. Claridge brought up a hex wrench with a torque reader on top of it, slipped it down over the post of the pressure coupling.

"Gently! Gently!" Barkley said. "You snap that off and we're dead." It was probably a bit of an overstatement: either they would be frozen by the liquid nitrogen, or boiled shortly thereafter by the series of ruptures in the cooling system which would immediately ensue. *Six of one, half a dozen of the other, really.* . . .

The ersatz Claridge glanced up at him, glanced away, and began to tighten the stopcock.

"That's it. Tighten it until that pointer on the torque meter hits that red line."

Claridge checked the torque meter. It was hard to turn in a confined space. . . . He checked the meter again, turned. The squeaking noises got louder as the torque on the part got greater, but slowly, slowly, the hissing of venting N_2 started to die away. Finally it stopped altogether, and the air around them began to clear a little as the frozen fog of the liquid nitrogen dispersed.

Barkley sagged a little bit. Claridge looked up at him and said, "You see? I told you we'd make a good team."

The smile was not entirely Claridge's, and Barkley hated the sight of it. *Solve one problem,* he thought, *and you're left with another.* . . .

He turned away.

Back up in the bridge, Claridge was in his accustomed place, working with the machinery as if everything were fine, as if there had been no change in standard operating procedure. . . . Barkley hauled himself up the ladder and sat down wearily in his place.

"Ed," Claridge said, "it won't be much longer. You've got to hold on and get us home."

Barkley looked at him coolly. "It's not your damned home!"

Claridge gazed back at him. The expression said, *It will be soon.*

Barkley stared, then turned away. "Did we lose A/C again?"

Claridge shook his head. "Cabin temp is stable at 80 degrees. You probably have a fever."

Barkley looked at Claridge with renewed paranoia. "Oh, is that what it is? Or is it one of your spores floating around in my body? Just what *does* that feel like?"

"It's painless. You wouldn't feel it at all. I assure you, whatever you're feeling has nothing to do with me."

Barkley turned and walked away. "We've only got a few hours until splashdown," said Claridge. "Ed, you can make it. Think about how much you want to see home again."

A voice spoke abruptly out of the air, and they both looked up in near-shock. "Mars 3, this is Houston, do you read?"

Apparently the work that Claridge had been doing on the comms had paid off. A flicker, and Megan's face appeared on screen. She looked drawn: the shirt was rumpled, the tie was askew, and she had somehow lost the suspenders. "Houston, thank God!" Barkley said. "I thought our comm was out completely."

"It's great to see your face, Mr. Barkley." She looked at him with such total and undisguised relief that he decided then and there that he was going to give her a rest from teasing for a good while now.

"It's great to be seen, Houston," Barkley said, and meant it more than he usually did.

"We have someone who wants to say hello to Dr. Claridge," said Megan.

On the screen, looking over Megan's shoulder, suddenly there were two faces that Barkley recognized: Claridge's wife, Jenny, and their little daughter, who was six.

"Pete?" his wife said. "Honey, are you OK?"

"I'm doing great, sweetheart!"

"Daddy!" the little girl said. "I lost my front teeth!"

"That's terrific, pumpkin," Claridge said smoothly. "You can tell me all about it when I see you."

He glanced across at Barkley, then up at the screen again. Barkley watched him, silent. Here was this total stranger who nonetheless knew Claridge's life, Claridge's secrets; he knew about the cabin, and the striped bass; he knew what Claridge's wife was like in bed, probably, and what pet names he called his child. . . . This creature could be anyone undetected, Barkley realized.

And how long had he been undetected, indeed, among three men who had become so close—as they had had little choice but to become. A year constantly in one another's company, enforced, inescapable. Required reading, while training for this mission, had been books written by Terry Waite and Brian Keenan, on what it was like to be kept prisoner in small confined spaces. At least they had the advantage that none of them were holding the others in duress.

Until now. . . .

"We have so much to catch up on," Jenny said.

"We'll be home real soon. I love you so much."

"I love you too. . . ."

Claridge smiled at the screen, and then, perhaps feeling the pressure of Barkley's eyes on him, looked across, and away again.

Barkley looked away from him, looked at the photo of the Three Musketeers, taped up on his monitor.

"What happened up there?" said Megan's voice. "Where is Commander Wells?"

Claridge got up from his post, came around toward Barkley's, and reached down for the button to kill the comms. "Just a moment, Houston," he said calmly, "you're breaking up. . . ."

While the screen was showing nothing but snow, he looked down at Barkley. "If you tell them about me . . . you know they'll abort the landing, and we'll die up here. They won't know me like you do. They won't know my good intentions. . . ."

Barkley could have choked at the sound of that, but for the time being he kept his opinion to himself.

"Don't you want it to be your decision whether to abort? Because if we don't land . . . it will be suicide for both of us."

Barkley sat very still. It was, of course, the worst place to hit any astronaut: the desire for control. It had been an issue ever since the Mercury designers had told the astronauts they couldn't have a window in their space capsule: since the USSR had built the first *Buran,* a space shuttle with a difference—flown entirely by remote control, from the ground, because its builders were afraid that a pilot might one day decide to land it in a country with a different political system, or a different base wage for astronauts.

No matter. Control was what it came down to, finally. It was like Claridge, too, to raise the issue . . . or like something living inside Claridge's memories and thinking processes.

Claridge's hand reached down, hit the button. "Houston . . . you there? Megan?"

The screen flickered: her image came back. "We read you. You were saying? . . ."

"Yes. I was saying that the best we could tell, we were hit by a micrometeorite. Al was. . . ."

"Al was injured," Claridge said.

"Is he OK? Where is he?"

"He's incapacitated," said Claridge again, so smoothly. "But don't worry, he's stable."

"What is the extent of your damage?" Megan said.

"Substantial. We're praying that this bucket holds together."

"We're tracking your progress on the big board. Switch your prior guidance system to auto and leave the driving to us."

The image of the probe as a giant Greyhound bus was briefly amusing. But, fortunately, the we-drive-you option wasn't open. "No can do, Houston," Barkley said. "That system's down. We've got to bring her in manually."

"Okay. We'll be back at you in a few minutes with your reentry vectors."

The screen flickered out. Claridge, with a slight smile, walked back around to his post, seated himself, and started working at the computer again

"You know," Barkley said, "as soon as we touch down, I'll tell them."

"Of course," said Claridge. "I'd expect nothing else."

"They'll probably isolate you and study you."

Claridge glanced at him. "I'm prepared for that."

Yes, Barkley thought, *I just bet you are....*

He looked once again at the picture taped to the monitor. That had always been Claridge's way: always prepared, the ultimate Boy Scout. He was even in one of those strange Scout secret societies with a secret handshake and classified merit badges. But it didn't matter: it was never Claridge's way to hold that over your head.... He held it as he held everything else in life: as a kind of hobby, everything amusing, and looked at in a kindly way. Except that the face looking at him from across the console now was not a kindly one. There was an unaccustomed grimness in the set of the jaw. Its owner was intent . . . and watching him, to see what he would do.

The screen flickered once more, and Megan's face came back again. She glanced up at one of her own monitors and said, "Your trajectory is almost perfect. You need to trim your burn five percent and then keep your speed constant. Splashdown will occur at 0530, two hundred miles northwest of Hawaii."

"Thanks, Megan," Barkley said. "I could use a few months on the beach."

"Roger that, Mr. Barkley . . . so could we all."

The beach. . . . He put the thought away. He couldn't believe he wasn't going to hear one of those damn alarms again.

"You're drifting out of line," Megan said, her voice sharp.

"Engage the right booster! Five sec burn!"

Barkley hit the button for the boost. The long virtual hallway down which the craft was making its way wavered from one side to the other as the probe's path wavered. This was no news: in simulator work, when you had to do a manual final injection, there was always a little jockeying to be done, a little "rough stuff" until the course smoothed out. And of course your reflexes were never quite as good as the computer's: there was always that magic tenth of a second between the moment it wanted you to hit the button and the moment you really did it. It had to do with the speed of thought inside the body, or of neuroelectricity, and about that, there was nothing to be done except try to compensate. . . .

He joysticked the booster venturi a little bit, watching the flight path.

"Come on, come on . . ." said Claridge. It was the same voice that had urged on a football team, the same voice from which he had won a hundred bucks . . . except that it wasn't the same man.

"You are back in pattern," Megan said. "Try to hold it, Ed."

He glanced up at the photo. Three of them, together. Pete's face kindly; Al's face, a little waspish, but amused, the way he always seemed to be; and in the middle, Barkley. Wondering, at the time of the picture, whether any of them would survive.

Now he knew.

"Come on . . ." said Claridge. "We're going to make it! I knew you could do it." His eyes glinted. But the triumph in them was the wrong kind for Pete, and there was something sleazy and insincere about the support. Claridge's always felt like a rock, plain and solid. But this rock was sand underneath, changeable, not to be depended upon. . . .

"Keep her on line for thirty more seconds," Megan said, "and gravity will do the rest. Twenty-six. Twenty-five. . . ."

Barkley's eyes lingered on Claridge, and then went back to the picture.

"That's it. Nineteen. Eighteen. . . ."

And it all became clear, as the attitude boosters roared, and the craft shook and moaned, and things, as always during burns, felt particularly vulnerable, ready to go wrong.

All the joshing talk about heroism that Claridge had so adroitly taken up. . . . It was not something to which Barkley had given much serious thought. Certainly it would be too easy to take the present definition of hero as gospel: someone who was publicly honored, who received tickertape parades and did the lecture circuits and got the big book advances, and was given standing ovations by people simply because he was still standing up and breathing after having had "a hard time, somewhere a long way off."

But in the old days, the definition of the word had been differently constituted. In those days, heroes who survived had been the exception, not the rule.

And now his own situation was plain, and clear, and it almost made him smile to realize it. No ticker-tape, no lectures, no books. . . .

But what remained was the one part of the equation that mattered. He remembered a definition he had read a long time ago: heroism was made of 90 percent fear, and 10 percent the ability to decide—and adding, almost as an afterthought, that it was worth looking at the etymology of the word 'decide,' since it meant 'to kill something'—a set of choices, a group of possibilities. It could be more than that, too. . . .

"Looking good," Megan said. "Ten . . . nine . . . eight. . . ."

On the screen they could see it: the sweet blue curve of Earth, with the delicate skin of atmosphere, translucent as silver leaf, laid over it all. No more red dust: instead, blue water, a beach somewhere, sun . . . no more cold dry winds. He had had enough of those, culminating in the chill that sat, watching, across the console from him.

It would taint the earth, if it got the chance. *Unavoidable.* In his mind Barkley saw the blue go blue-gray, cold and dusty. Not in reality: the weather wouldn't change. But what sat across from him would spread. And the choice, the decision . . . sat in front of him.

"Seven . . . six . . . five. . . ."

And Barkley pushed the joystick control right over to the side.

He could feel the change in the thrust, the protesting rockets pushing him and the probe off to one side. Claridge, staring at the screen, reacted in horror as the virtual "pathway" of their course went askew again. The ship broke right through that virtual wall and out the other side—

"What are you doing?" Claridge shouted.

"The capsule is offline!" Megan shouted, urgent, from the screen. "I repeat, the capsule is offline—"

Barkley stared straight ahead of him, seeing the straight path . . . not the curving course home, now decaying. Seeing the way to go . . . though not home.

Claridge got up, headed for him. "You don't know what you're doing!"

"I know exactly what *you're* doing—we splash down, and before I can turn you in to the authorities, you procreate me and throw my dead body into the ocean!"

"I have no intention of doing that!"

Liar, Barkley thought.

As Claridge came toward him, Barkley got up out of his seat, and Claridge ignored him, immediately sitting down in the seat and starting to try to correct the course. He paid no attention to Barkley behind him.

Too single-minded, Barkley thought. *Never one of the real Claridge's problems. He was always going off on tangents. . . .* He picked up that blessed fire extinguisher, and with it hit the manual control for the inner EVA bay door, smashing it. Sparks flew from the control: when requested, for a change.

The doors slid open as something shorted out violently. The dust rose and flew all over again as air rushed out into the space. Claridge turned, stared at him, horrified. But Barkley was standing by the door, and his hand was on the emergency release for the outer door.

"Ed," said Claridge carefully, "that will depressurize the cabin . . . we'll both be blown to pieces."

"That's right," Ed said, in triumph.

"Claridge's" eyes narrowed. "My species is millions of years old. It's our right to take life so that we may continue to exist."

It was a claim his own species had made, though rarely mentioning millions of years when they did it. In any case, now, at the last moment, the other's true colors showed. Well, Ed had been expecting it. "Then they'll have to find someone else to carry the torch," he said with satisfaction, "because *your* existence is about to be discontinued."

Claridge reached out toward him, and the change began. The awful green chitinous form overtaking the human, the awful alien shriek beginning to fill the cabin as the creature lurched toward him, tentacles reaching—

This time Barkley did not back away. He was not surprised. He knew what to expect—and for an astronaut, after all, that was nine-tenths of the game.

He hit the switch.

The decompression hit him. Barkley let it happen: opened his mouth, let the big sneeze come, felt the blood boil up, opened the eyes and let the eyeballs mist over and crackle with the beginnings of ice; knowing that in a matter of a second, the fire would bloom and end it all—

They were close enough to Earth that some people actually saw it as a naked-eye incident: a brief pinprick of fire in the sky. NORAD predicted the path of impact of most of the fragments. Many of them came down in the Pacific, causing it to rain stars over the beaches of the Big Island of Hawaii. Some caused a brief track of daylight meteors and bolides over the Midwest.

The ensuing investigation would go on for years. No one would ever really understand what happened.

And one piece of wreckage would never come down. It was found, much later, by a shuttle crew up to do work on the Hubble Space Telescope, but it would not have been indicative either. It was a picture, somewhat charred around the edges, freeze-dried and a little brittle, but otherwise well preserved after its long sojourn in the cold and the dark—a photo of three men, one with a dark and kind face; one a little narrow-faced and waspish, but wearing a smile; and a third, big and blunt-faced and ironic-looking, who at least died knowing he was still who he had been a few hours before. None of those who found the picture would recognize him as a hero.

But it would not matter. For one type of hero is the one who lays down his life in the knowledge that those he saves will never know. . . .

DIANE DUANE has published more than twenty science fiction and fantasy novels and has developed Star Trek *stories in more media than any other author. Duane also writes extensively for the screen. She has written more than forty animation scripts for every animation studio, including the memorable episode "Where No One Has Gone Before" for* Star Trek: The Next Generation.

As David Schow points out in his introduction, this episode was originally intended as the pilot of a new series—a spin-off from the original Outer Limits *to be called* The Unknown. *As such, it has a somewhat more fantastical tone than most episodes. And the story itself has everything: sex, madness, poetry, intrigue, gothic horror, a cacophony of clocks, a mysterious return from the dead—and more!*

The Forms of Things Unknown

Adaptation by Richard A. Lupoff
Original Screenplay by Joseph Stefano

He stood on a small grass-covered rise, gazing over the surface of the lake. The water was dark, reflecting little of the dim, cloud-shrouded afternoon sky. What light there was, seemed almost to be leached from the stands of black, autumnal trees that surrounded the body of water.

Here and there an insect skimmed the unmoving plane of water. Once a bird call could be heard, the haunting, mournful song of a loon, but the source of the bird call was nowhere to be seen.

The man had the youthful good looks of one whose breeding went back centuries, who had been nourished and pampered throughout his life. Not yet thirty years of age, an acute observer might recognize that he would run to fat in later life. Fat and the subtly unpleasant appearance of moral corruption that both precedes and presages physical breakdown.

His clothing lay nearby in a heap. Raising his arms, as if gathering the resolve to challenge an icy bath, and permitting a single laugh to escape his lips, he raced down the grassy slope and into the water. He moved with the elegance of a natural athlete, his feet finding a firm purchase on the lake's bottom. Then one foot struck a slippery spot, perhaps a submerged stone covered with mossy slime.

His expression changed from smug self-gratification to panic, but only for an instant. He regained his footing and with it his confidence. More cautiously now he strode forward along the gently sloping lake bed, toward the irregular black trees that marked the distant limit of the lake.

Once more he paused, turned and peered back toward the shore and the grassy rise. He frowned, less with displeasure than with petulance.

Beyond the grassy rise, barely visible from the man's position in the lake, stood a gleaming automobile. A Rolls Royce Silver Ghost, it had obviously been maintained with loving care and with no regard for expense. To the eye, it would have been impossible to tell how long the Rolls had stood in this place, but an acute ear might have heard the low, distinctive tick of a cooling engine. The car could have been in place only a matter of minutes.

He called, "Kassia! Leonora!"

There was no response.

He repeated, "Kassia!"

And, "Leonora!"

Inside the Silver Ghost, Kassia Paine held her eyes on the work her hands were performing. She had opened the car's fully stocked bar. She wore a new Givenchy sheath of white linen. The lines and the color of the sheath seemed made to complement her perfect skin and honey-blond hair. The dress lay close against her splendid slim figure, good enough for a salon model, and in fact she had pursued that occupation for several years in her native New York. But her role now was a more lucrative one, if also more dubious, than that of mannequin.

Kassia stirred the ingredients of a martini. In keeping with the chill of the afternoon, the frigid liquor in the graceful, blown-glass shaker seemed more liquid ice than gin and vermouth.

She might have heard the man's repeated call, "Kassia," but she gave no evidence of having done so.

Not fifty feet from the Rolls—and a little farther from the edge of the lake—a second woman knelt before a peculiar shrub. Like Kassia, Leonora Edmond was clad in a form-fitting sheath, but hers was of black linen, also complementing the rose-porcelain of her skin and the darkness of her hair.

The shrub was covered with peculiar leaves: long and slender and pointed like stilettos. The bush itself was thorny, and Leonora worked carefully in the dimming afternoon light, trying to remove a single leaf from the shrub without a vicious thorn scratching or piercing her delicate skin.

She heard her name called, "Leonora!" and winced, barely escaping a wound. She bit her lip in concentration, managed to removed a single deadly leaf from the shrub, and rose to her feet. As she did so, the male voice demanded, with an almost audible pout and pause between each word and its successor, "Where's . . . my . . . drink?"

Leonora brushed a twig from her knee, trotted to the Rolls, and carefully delivered the single black leaf to the other woman.

Kassia accepted the leaf with as much care as Leonora had exercised in gathering it. She removed the domed metal lid from the glass martini shaker, dropped in the leaf, resealed the shaker, and agitated the mixture. Kassia smiled, thinking, If the vermouth was bruised by the process, she would put it in its place. Leonora watched the process with a look of anguish and, perhaps, of guilt.

Now Kassia opened the shaker, removed the black leaf with care, and handed it to Leonora. Soon it was disposed of, ground beneath the sole of Leonora's expensive shoe; both women had been careful to handle it as little as possible, and to wipe their fingers carefully after any touch.

And again the male voice was heard. "Am I or am I not going to get that drink?"

Kassia turned to face the source of the voice. Although the thick trees and rounded earth cut off her view of the man standing in the lake, she whispered, "Yes, André, you are."

She turned back and caught a glimpse of Leonora holding her fingers to her lips in the manner of a frightened, guilt-stricken child. Instantly, Kassia slapped the other woman's hand away from her face. In a whisper marked by urgent disapproval she hissed, "Do you want to poison yourself to death?"

She climbed from the Rolls, the martini shaker in one hand, a fan-shaped, slim-stemmed martini glass in the other. Leonora scrambled to remove herself from Kassia's path.

André's position, a score of yards from the lake shore, still provided a clear view of the grassy rise. He stood up to his knees in chill water but seemed unconcerned by its bite. He jammed his hands to his narrow hips, chin held arrogantly high, gazing impatiently toward the shore.

Then he smiled.

Light-haired, smooth-skinned Kassia had appeared. She topped the rise and walked carefully toward the lake. She managed somehow to maintain a model's poise and balance despite walking in stiletto heels on the grass. She held the shaker in one hand, the empty martini glass in the other, temptingly.

She asked, "Must you go wading in that abominable water?"

André grinned, then, sarcastically, he whispered, "That isn't my drink you have there, is it?"

From beside the Rolls, Leonora watched and listened with the alert attention of a nervous doe.

Kassia smiled at André, unspeaking.

He barked, "Bring it here."

Kassia remained motionless.

André snapped his fingers in angry command. "I told you, bring it here." he tilted his head, peering beyond Kassia, toward the clearing where he knew the Rolls had been parked. "Leonora?"

There was no response but André knew the two women well enough, knew their vulnerabilities and needs and weaknesses, to play them like two musical instruments. One like a brazen horn, one like a delicate viola.

But it was not André who spoke, it was Kassia. "Come here, Leonora."

Leonora advanced from the car to the grassy rise. She picked her way carefully to Kassia's side. She waited for the next word, the next event.

"Give her the glass, Kassia." André nodded imperatively.

Kassia complied. Leonora clutched the martini glass by its slim stem. Kassia held the shaker now in both her hands.

"Now," André continued, "Both of you. Bring me my drink. Kassia will pour. Leonora will serve." He paused, then resumed: "And come as you are! In your fine stiletto heels." He laughed, the only one amused by his joke.

He waited, never doubting that the two women would obey his commands, however demeaning, however irrational they might be.

Kassia advanced first, her expensive shoes plunging into the shallow water and silted lake bed. With each step the water rose, to the hem of her pale sheath, to the knee, to the thighs. She could sense Leonora behind her, hear Leonora's gasp as the icy water rose higher and higher on her legs. Her midnight linen sheath would look as black as the water in the falling dusk, but Kassia did not turn to watch.

Instead, she held her gaze fixed on André as he backed away from her, retreating into deeper and deeper water.

Somewhere beyond the horizon thunder rolled across the darkening springtime sky. Thunderstorms were common in summer, in this part of France, but were almost unknown this early in the year.

A cold wind rippled the surface of the lake, and black leaves, remnants of the previous autumn's denuding of the branches, skimmed its surface before dropping to the water.

Again, André issued his command. "Kassia will pour. Leonora will serve."

He seemed to consider his plans. Unsmiling, almost solemn, while he waited for his. . . . His what? Servants? Whores? Demimondaines? Yes, *demimondaines*. The word had a nice ring to it, antique and somewhat ambiguous; a very good word.

He waited for his chatelaines to comply with their instructions, and then he said, as much to himself as to the two women, "And then we'll go to London. We'll cross the channel and pay a dark call on

Leonora's rich and respected father. And when we've extorted him we'll leave London. Not very respected, but very rich."

It could not have been brightness; in the fading light, anything but. Still, Leonora squeezed her eyes shut as she extended the martini glass toward Kassia.

Kassia uncapped the sweating blown-glass shaker, tilted the shaker, watched with total concentration as the clear liquid with its faint suggestion of oiliness provided by the dash of vermouth flowed smoothly into the glass. She made an almost undetectable sound to let Leonora know that she was finished pouring.

Leonora opened her eyes, raised her arm and swung it carefully toward André. He accepted the glass without offering any sign of gratitude or even acknowledgment, and raised it to his lips. He tilted the glass, smiled again to himself rather than to either woman, and slowly, carefully, drained the glass. By the time he finished the drink he had tilted his head back and might have been watching a storm cloud, as thick and black as roiling smoke, as it writhed above him.

Kassia watched carefully, then tilted the blown-glass martini shaker and poured all that remained of its contents into the icy lake water.

André ignored the women. He held his eyes fixed on the clouds overhead. The glass remained poised above his mouth, and a few straggling drops of clear liquid rolled down the glass, to the rim, and to his eager, sensuous lips.

Slowly he lowered his head, lowering the glass, also, from his lips. He smiled at the two women, more as one would smile at a fondly held possession than at a human being. One might imagine him smiling like this at the Rolls Silver Ghost when he first took possession of it.

He let the martini glass slip from between his fingers; it made a soft sound as it struck the water, hardly causing a splash. Oddly, it did not sink but remained floating, bobbing like a child's wooden boat. Still smiling to himself, André placed his hands softly against his youthful flat abdomen.

Then, as if he had remembered some horrifying event of long ago, some happening suppressed in childhood and shockingly, frighteningly recalled decades later, his expression altered. The gentle grin of self-satisfied pleasure turned to a grotesque rictus. He opened his mouth wide, drew in a deep lungful of air, held it for a fleeting moment, then slowly released it.

His hands, still flat against his belly, gripped convulsively as if to rip out the flesh from his ribs to his groin. He emitted a single abrupt yell, which echoed across the flat surface of the lake, and plunged forward, face down, crashing through the surface of the lake as if it had been a sheet of perfect glass or a layer of almost invisible ice no thicker than a playing card.

As he thrashed in the cold water the two women stood watching. There would be no point in their hurrying back to the lake's edge, to the grassy rise. Their pumps and sheaths were both muddied and drenched; in all likelihood, ruined beyond reclamation. They might as well remain in place until the drama was completed.

With a final convulsion, André relapsed face-down into the water; if the contents of his drink did not kill him, then the immersion in the lake surely would.

The martini glass bobbed away from André's outstretched, twitching hand. Kassia leaned forward and lifted it. She shook a few droplets from its base. She advanced from the lake, passing Leonora and handing her the glass and shaker. Behind her a chilly, errant wind stirred the lake once more.

Having handed the glass and shaker to Leonora, Kassia waded back to André's body. It was easy to tow the floating body to the edge of the lake, more difficult to drag it across the grassy bank. She saw Leonora standing, watching horrified, the glass and shaker still in her hands.

"Put those things back in the bar," Kassia directed. "Then open the car trunk. Take out bags and put them on the back seat. And leave the trunk open."

The Silver Ghost rolled down the darkening country road, its engine whispering, its tires crunching now and then on rocks or twigs. Kassia gripped the wheel confidently as she guided the big car steadily beneath overarching branches. Leonora huddled in the passenger seat, her face turned downward, arms covering her head as if she were a boxer defending against an overwhelming onslaught.

Kassia slammed on the Rolls's brakes and the car skidded to a halt, throwing up a hail of pebbles and sticks. The car had reached a country crossroads.

A funeral procession was crossing before the Rolls. The coffin was mounted on a hand-drawn cart. The mourners were few, and mostly aged, but one young woman in widow's weeds trudged beside the makeshift catafalque, a small funerary bouquet clutched to her breast. As the procession passed the Rolls, the young widow cast a bitter, hopeless glance at the clouded sky. She lowered her glance to the car and hurled some bit of dark vegetation.

The leaf or petal struck the Rolls's windscreen at the same moment as the first heavy drop of spring rain. Kassia switched on the wipers. The procession passed out of sight. She slipped the car into gear and it moved forward.

Later the car reached a fork in the back road. Full night had fallen now, and the overcast night sky provided no illumination of moon or stars; the Rolls's headlamps made twin tunnels through the rural blackness. A sign beside the road read, *Aix-Les-Bains—43 kilometres.*

Kassia glanced at Leonora. The Englishwoman was curled in the farthermost corner of the passenger seat, sleeping the light, troubled sleep of the mentally and physically exhausted. Holding one hand on the steering wheel, Kassia reached over with the other and gave her companion a small, sharp shove.

Leonora woke with a gasp.

"Light me a cigarette, Leonora," Kassia commanded.

Leonora felt for the crumpled pack of cigarettes that she knew should be on the seat. Her eyes were fixed in horrified fascination on the car's rear-view mirror. She found the cigarettes, removed one from the package with unfeeling, zombie-like fingers, and reached for the dashboard lighter. But before she could find the lighter she dropped the cigarette, her mouth wide with terror.

"He isn't dead," she gasped, and then, almost in a scream, again, "He isn't dead!"

Staring horrified into the rear-view mirror, she was able to see the Rolls's trunk lid slowly rising. The mirror was so angled that, from the passenger seat, she would not normally have seen what she did. But when she leaned to press the dashboard lighter, the image in the mirror had caught her attention.

Behind the wheel, Kassia raised her eyes involuntarily to the mirror. She slammed on the brakes and the Rolls skidded to a halt at the edge of the little-traveled road.

"He has to be," Kassia whispered. "We poisoned him. That one leaf would have murdered a whole world of Andrés."

"No." For once, Leonora found the strength to disagree. "Men like André Pavan don't die until they want to." She shriveled farther into her corner of the car, as if the upholstery might swallow her up once and for all, and as if she would welcome such strange oblivion.

Swinging the Rolls's heavy driver's-side door open, Kassia stepped to the muddy roadway and made her way to the rear of the car. The trunk lid was unlatched and had risen a few inches from its closed position. It might have wavered slightly even as Kassia watched, fascinated, or that might have been a trick of the failing illumination. Kassia curled her fingers under the edge of the trunk lid and lifted. The lid swung up easily.

André lay within, folded like a garden chair to fit into the trunk. His face was turned away from Kassia. His graceful body lay as it had been when Kassia dragged it from the lake. Alongside it lay André's expensive slacks, his silk sports shirt, black blazer, and Italian hand-woven sandals.

Kassia stood motionless, staring at the body, as motionless as André. Finally she called, "Leonora?"

Through the Rolls's rear window, Kassia could see her companion, sitting up now, staring at her in the rearview mirror.

"Come here, Leonora," Kassia commanded.

The other woman obeyed, sliding across the leather-covered seats, behind the wheel, through the driver's-side door. Tentatively, she made her way to Kassia's side. She stood, icily paralyzed by the moment.

As if she had been a kindergarten teacher reasoning with an irrationally terrified child, Kassia said, "See for yourself. He is dead."

Leonora said, "All right." Happy to accept her companion's word, unwilling to look into the trunk, she started back toward the car door.

Kassia whirled and grasped Leonora's arm. "You'll feel better if you see for yourself."

Leonora yielded. As soon as Kassia loosened her grasp on her arm, she stood at the open trunk, steeled herself and opened her eyes. She stared, stared, and then without preface exclaimed, "He blinked!"

Before Kassia could react, Leonora bolted.

Within the trunk, André's face was now turned toward Kassia. His eyes were closed. He did not move. Kassia called, "Leonora!" The other woman had disappeared into the woods beside the rural road. With an angry word, Kassia returned to the passenger compartment and found a flashlight. She would have to find Leonora.

Although there was no visible sign of Leonora's passage, her gasping exhalations and crashing progress through trees and shrubs permitted Kassia to pursue her.

Half exhausted, fully terrified, Leonora tumbled over a fallen tree trunk. Before she could rise and resume her flight, Kassia caught up with her. She stood over the fallen woman, shining the flashlight on her.

"Get up. We have to go."

Leonora pushed herself upright, leaned against a tree. "No. I can't, Kassia. You go with him. Help him do what he intended to do. Tell my father I won't debase him by asking him to forgive me."

Kassia shook her head. "Your father will be safe now, Leonora. André is dead."

Leonora composed her words as carefully as if they were a judge's pronouncement of death. "He blinked."

"No, Leonora, he could not have blinked."

"And I remember the position he was in. My—my soul photographed it just before you closed the trunk. So I remember. His face was turned the other way."

Kassia grimaced. "*I* moved it. Just a moment ago. To make certain he wasn't alive."

After a lengthy silence, Leonora said, "And he wasn't?"

"No. He was not alive."

In the distance, behind Kassia, spring lightning flashed. Leonora blinked against the sudden brightness. Was that—was it the silhouette of a man? Kassia responded to Leonora's own reaction, but as she turned the illumination faded and only woods stood before her.

Desperately, Leonora raced through the woods, miraculously finding her way back to the Rolls. She stood beside its open trunk, the back of one hand pressed against her trembling mouth, her teeth gnawing at her own flesh. Her eyes stared in terror.

The trunk was empty.

Kassia brushed past her, eyes fixed on the open door of the Rolls. She plunged inside, slammed the driver's-side door shut, and wiped the rain from her eyes.

She started the engine.

Later, after struggling through blackness and rain, the Rolls came to a halt before a looming building. The road had twisted and turned maddeningly, until Kassia had lost all sense of direction and all concept of time. The structure stood at the end of a private driveway. It was visible only through the intervention of more flashes of lightning. Kassia swung the big car off the roadway and onto the private drive.

For just a moment Kassia had lost her composure, and now she realized that she had abandoned her companion on the roadway. For all her failings, Leonora was vital to Kassia's plans. And now she was somewhere on the rural road. Kassia considered swinging the Rolls back out onto the road and searching, but finally decided to seek help from the occupants of the building.

Once more lightning flashed. In its fleeting brilliance Kassia could see the building before her. It was a château, typical of the French countryside. Small for its type, yet speaking of some wealthy citizen's desire to show off his success to the world at large.

Lights were visible inside the château, and a lantern-like fixture blazed beside the front door.

Kassia gasped as she recognized the black-clad figure standing at that door, pounding her fists helplessly against the wood, crying out, "Please! Let me in! Help me! Please!"

How was it possible? Kassia had abandoned Leonora on the road. There was no way that Leonora could have covered the distance more rapidly on foot than Kassia had driven, nor had Kassia seen Leonora anywhere *en route*. But if the Englishwoman had cut through the woods, striking a direct course to the château while Kassia had doubled back and forth on the winding road, maybe she could have cut the distance traveled dramatically.

Again, Leonora cried, "Please! Help me!"

Kassia all but leaped from the big car. She covered the yards that separated her from Leonora in rapid strides. Approaching from the rear, she clapped her hand over Leonora's mouth, whispering fiercely, "Do you want to tell the world what we've done? And why we had to do it?"

Leonora slumped backward, almost collapsing in Kassia's arms.

The château's door swung open. In the doorway stood a figure, bathed in the illumination of a flagstone-floored foyer. The man was bald and elderly, garbed in the collarless, high-necked jacket common to servants and housemen in the region. In the illumination of the foyer, his staring sightless eyes made his condition unmistakable.

He had responded to Leonora's pounding and pleading. Now he asked, "Are you in trouble?"

Before Leonora could speak, Kassia said, "Our car broke down. We managed to struggle along to this château, but it won't go any farther. We wondered if we could telephone a garage."

The blind eyes stared straight ahead but the old man's expression was kindly. "We have no telephone," he said. "My Mr. Hobart is not interested in communicating with anyone capable of responding."

He stepped aside, sensing the condition of the women. "If you will lead me to your car, I will bring your luggage to the château. You are wet, you must change your clothing." He gestured, "Welcome to our loneliness."

The old man identified himself only as Colas. Kassia guided him to the Rolls and he carried their bags from the back seat to the château.

With Leonora all but collapsing against her, she returned to the château and stepped into the foyer.

Instantly she was assaulted by the din of uncounted clocks, ticking and clacking in mad disharmony. Where they were was as unclear as what they meant. She tried to shut them out of her mind, but there must have been hundreds of them. No, thousands if not tens of thousands.

What madman would fill a château with timepieces and then set them all ticking away, to create this clattering cacophony?

With Leonora on her arm Kassia followed Colas down a long hallway. The floor was all of flagstone. The walls were of ancient masonry. The ceiling was vaulted and beamed. The sound of the clocks was everywhere.

Colas turned and fixed his eerie, sightless eyes on the women. "Permit me to show you to a changing room. If you will leave your wet clothing there, I will tend to it presently."

In the relative quiet of the changing room they toweled off and changed from their soaked outfits to dry clothing from their luggage. Sitting on the edge of a bed, her hair wrapped in a towel and clad only in fresh underwear, Leonora held a loose end of the towel to her eyes and sobbed.

"What's the matter?" Kassia stood over her, in similar dishabille. She planted her fists on her rounded hips in unconscious parody of André's sometime demanding posture. "What are you wailing about now?"

Leonora uncovered her eyes and raised them to her companion. "What we did. We—"

"We did what we had to do. Only that, nothing more."

"But—to kill."

Kassia did not speak.

"Did we really have to do it?" Leonora asked.

Kassia shook her head. "You know the answer to that. He said he wanted to go ahead with the scheme, but you know that he had no intention of sharing with us, as we'd planned. Once André had his hands on your father's money, we'd never have seen him again. I know the type, Leonora. I've worked with them before."

"It was my fault, wasn't it?" Leonora stood up and rubbed the thick towel vigorously over her hair. "I should never have introduced him to you. I should never have introduced *myself.* I just—I saw you there on the runway, and you were everything I'd always wanted to be. Beautiful, poised, so sure of yourself. And when you caught my eye and smiled at me, I was thrilled. I thought, she's come all the way from America and here she is in this show, and she's smiled at a nobody like me."

Kassia frowned. "You're no nobody, my dear."

"And then when you came to the house and my father laid eyes on you—he'd never gotten over

Mother, you know. Never. Until he met you. And then he was like a moonstruck schoolboy. At his age. I can hardly blame him, but then he wrote those letters."

There was a gentle, almost diffident knock at the door.

Kassia called, "Yes?"

Colas, in his soft voice, asked if there was anything further they might like.

Kassia said, "No, we're almost ready, we'll be right there." When they did leave the changing room they found Colas waiting in patient silence. He led them down a narrow hallway, past a winding staircase whose upper reaches disappeared into looming darkness. The house's illumination emanated chiefly from the second-floor hallway, spilling like flowing water down another staircase into the lower hallway.

Kassia and Leonora stood in the center of the stone floor, their ears assaulted by the overwhelming clatter of uncounted clocks pouring from above.

Colas crossed the area with the serene confidence of a blind person functioning in totally familiar surroundings. Beside a pair of heavy wooden doors he reached for a key hanging from a wall fixture. He fitted it into a lock, twisted, and swung the doors back.

He stood aside to permit the two women to enter an archaic country-home parlor, then followed them in and closed the doors behind him.

The first thing that caught Kassia's eye, oddly, was little more than a trinket, a figurine of a woman less tall than Kassia's own upraised hand. She was fashioned of a darkened metal, perhaps copper or bronze, and was clad in a ballerina's graceful skirt and top. In her miniature hands she held a long pole, like the bamboo pole carried by a tightrope walker. The pole was weighted at the ends.

The ballerina stood *en pointe* on a raised metal platform no broader than the palm of a woman's hand. She was spinning on her pointed toe, reflecting the golden light that a blazing fire cast from a huge stone hearth at one side of the room.

Without a word, Colas crossed to the fireplace, knelt and gathered additional wood from an ornate bin. He bent over the fire and skillfully built it until its light and heat filled the room.

As he worked, Leonora moved from Kassia's side and stood gazing at a clock. Instead of numerals, the clock's face was painted with the face of a French circus clown. The clock was not part of the cacophony that filled the house. Its hands were bent and motionless.

Turning from his task, the old man stood facing Leonora. In some odd way he seemed to study her, despite his sightlessness. He smiled gently and said to her, "I wonder if others can see your beauty as I do."

Hearing the old man's words, Kassia tore her gaze away from the dancing figurine. She smiled at Colas's words, then said, "Sometimes it seems you *have* to be blind to see beauty."

Leonora blinked, like one startled out of a state of mental absorption. While her body had been in the room with Kassia, and the blind, gentle Colas, her mind had been absorbed by the tumultuous ticking and clattering of the clocks. In this room the sound was muffled, but still clearly audible.

She asked, "Where is it coming from?"

"The ticks of time?" Colas responded. "From upstairs. A special room upstairs."

"It sounds like a million mad clocks."

Colas smiled. He fed more dried wood to the warming blaze. Finally he said, "My Mr. Hobart tinkers with time . . . just as time has tinkered with Mr. Hobart."

Suddenly, shockingly, the shattering ticking sounds that provided a muffled background for their fragmented conversation rose to a clattering roar.

Leonora and Kassia whirled to face the double doors through which they had entered the parlor. A man stood silhouetted in the doorway, his hands outstretched, still holding the hammered copper handles of both doors.

Leonora's eyes widened with recognition—she had seen this man before!

Kassia observed the scene calmly, alertly, like a strong animal prepared either for combat or flight.

Without a word, the newcomer stepped back into the foyer, pulling the twin doors shut behind him. The ticking dropped to a tolerable level once again.

Kassia had neither to fight nor flee. She exhaled. Without taking her eyes from the doors, she asked Colas, "Who was that?"

With a bemused smile, Colas responded, "Who *could* it have been?"

Kassia, gathering her reserve of courage, strode purposefully to the doors. As she reached them she heard Leonora call out a single word, "No!" But she twisted the twin handles and pulled the doors open, admitting the roar of ticking and clattering once again.

She caught sight of the silhouetted man once more, for a fraction of a second. He stood with his hands on his slim hips, a frightening doppleganger of André as he had stood arrogantly in the black lake.

Watching from the parlor, Leonora staggered backward and collapsed onto a brocade-covered sofa, one of a pair that flanked the fireplace. Kassia had backed into the parlor as well, and the man stood silhouetted again in the opened doorway. Kassia stood as if paralyzed, Leonora lay stunned on the sofa; both of them stared at the man in the doorway.

Only Colas spoke, softly and caringly. "If you are wet, come and stand close to the fire."

The young man's hand barely touched the weighted balance pole of the tiny metallic dancer, but even the slightest push set her to twirling rapidly in the dancing firelight. The young man himself had a fragile handsomeness. His brow was wide and his eyes deep, with the brooding, introspective intensity seen in some portraits of the young Napoleon. His fine, almost albino hair swept high above his forehead, giving an almost angelic cast to his face in contradistinction to the saturnine, almost diabolical grace of André.

He swung his glance from the whirling dancer to the two women so recently arrived at the château and to the solicitous, fatherly, blind Colas. Leonora lay on the fireside sofa, covered now with a warm goose-down comforter. Kassia knelt beside her, for the moment ignoring the two men in the room, observing Leonora with mute anxiety. Colas had brought a decanter of brandy and a crystal snifter, and poured a generous tot into the snifter.

He replaced the decanter on the mantelpiece and held the glass toward Kassia, as certain of her position as if he had possessed utterly clear vision. As Kassia took the snifter, Colas, indicating Leonora, told her, "Put it to her lips."

While Kassia held the snifter to Leonora's mouth, Colas gently raised her head. She did not drink, but the warmth of Kassia's hands—and, perhaps, of the nearby flames—raised fumes from the brandy. As the fumes reached Leonora's nostrils, she opened her eyes and glanced across the room. In a great wooden chair, upholstered in the same fabric as the sofa where she lay, the blond man sat, calmly watching her.

He smiled. "Did you think I was someone else?"

Leonora whispered, "Yes."

"But she'd forgotten," Kassia interjected. "He's dead now."

More alert now, Leonora pushed herself to a semi-recumbent posture on the sofa. She accepted the brandy snifter from Kassia and held it close to her face. After a moment she sipped the fiery liquid, watching the dancing flames on the hearth through its golden lens. She sighed and closed her eyes. She lowered the snifter.

The blond man had left his seat and crossed the room to join the others. He accepted the snifter from Leonora's fingers. He spoke again, with the air and tone of one reciting a beloved but baffling verse.

"Such tricks hath a strong imagination that, if it would but apprehend some joy, it comprehends some bringer of that joy, or in the night, imagining some fear, how easy is a bush supposed a bear."

As swiftly as he had adopted his puzzling new manner he resumed his normal mien. Smiling, he asked, "What are you doing in this house?"

Leonora said nothing. Kassia rose to her feet, looking to Colas for guidance.

As if sensing her silent appeal, Colas explained, "I welcomed them in, Mr. Hobart."

"Could they leave at once?" Hobart responded. "Or will they spend the night?"

Leonora sat up straight. "We'll go now."

Kassia shook her head. "We'll spend the night." Perhaps she had remembered the lie of the failing automobile. Perhaps she had another reason. "Leonora will sleep on the sofa. And—see—there is its twin—I shall sleep there."

To the blond man she said, "Good night, Mr. Hobart."

The blond man turned toward Leonora. "My name is Tone Hobart. I think my parents meant to call me Anthony, or Antonio, or perhaps Anton, eh, as in the great composer Bruckner, but it came out as, simply, Tone. Please tell me your name."

Before Leonora could reply, Kassia said, "My friend is Leonora Edmond. I am Kassia Paine." She stood, studying his face, thinking of the odd words he had previously spoken. "Are you a poet?"

"Who else would quote Shakespeare in time of stress?" he asked. Then, "Have you known poets?"

She frowned. "No." And, after a silence filled only by the distant clattering of clocks, "Only lovers and madmen. But the lunatic, the lover, and the poet are of imagination all compact."

Tone Hobart smiled and offered an almost imperceptible nod to acknowledge the line snatched from the same source as his own citation. "I'm sorry," he said, "that I frightened you in the woods."

Kassia frowned in puzzlement.

"It was I," Hobart persisted. "Feel my hair. Still wet. From the rain."

Her hand moved almost of its own volition, to take him up on his offer. But she drew it back without touching him, and stood staring. Finally he smiled faintly, returned to the double doors, and placed his hands on the hammered handles. He paused there and spoke without looking back at the others.

"Please do not need me, or needlessly disturb me. I have a great deal of work to do tonight. Upstairs." The angled motion of his head indicated the direction of his last word. He pulled the doors wide and the clatter of the clocks rushed into the room, filling it with a sea of tiny, jagged sounds.

Colas rushed after Hobart, pausing at the entrance to the parlor to pull the twin doors shut behind him.

With the closing of the doors, the clatter fell away like a receding tide, leaving only the auditory detritus of a low, irritating ticking. Within the parlor, their bodies casting elongated shadows that danced like the whirling metal figurine before the leaping flames, Kassia and Leonora shared a chilling sense of aloneness.

Leonora pleaded. "We won't stay here, Kassia? We will go, won't we?" When Kassia refused to answer, she went on. "I feel as if . . . as if I shouldn't be here."

"Why?" Kassia asked calmly.

"It's as if—as if this house has been waiting for me. I—" She cast a pleading look at Kassia. "I'm afraid I'll succumb to it."

Kassia offered a small, possibly compassionate smile. "Genuinely susceptible people like you rarely succumb to anything." She tilted her head and smiled more openly. "Do you know why I didn't leave him in the lake? He would have floated into someone's life. Even in death, he'd find a way to betray us."

She crossed the parlor to the twin doors. She put her hand on one of them, then turned back toward Leonora. "This is the kind of neighborhood I was looking for. A good neighborhood for unmarked graves."

Tone Hobart climbed the stairway with a steady, almost mechanical stride, as if he were propelled by a clockwork engine. When he reached the head of the stairway he continued, neither faster nor slower, walking down a long, narrow hallway. Its walls were as white as death; its floor as chill as a tomb. Raw, cold illumination was provided by rows of naked light bulbs strung on ugly black wires.

At the end of the hallway he approached the door to his workshop. The clattering of clocks grew louder with each stride, and as he neared the room the clatter was joined by the angry roaring of an untamed wind.

The room must have been left unlocked, for as Hobart neared it the door swung open and a gust of cold, moisture-laden air swept out and past him. He stepped into the room, leaning against the onrushing watery wind, and slammed the door shut behind him.

The room was not large nor was it decorated or furnished save for Hobart's experimental equipment. There were no windows or doors other than the one through which he had entered. But there was a large, square opening in the ceiling; through it the black sky and scudding dark clouds could be seen. Through it the violent wind carried its burden of moisture.

The ceiling was low. The thousands of clocks that furnished the clattering noise were concentrated in this single room. They were of every size and variety, from giant grandfather clocks and huge display clocks that would have been more in place on the faces of commercial buildings, to tiny, ornate bedside timepieces that would have chimed the hours in the bedchambers of French nobility in the days of the *ancien régime*.

There were Spartan clocks with only simple hands and hour markers, and ornate clocks with scrollwork and graven angels with puffed-out cheeks and tiny, feathery wings, and playful clocks designed to hang in children's rooms, with cats' eyes set into their faces and cats' tails for pendulums.

A narrow path led through the ranks and masses of clocks, to a heavy black iron pole that rose from the room's floor through the opening in the roof. An insane spider web of black metallic wires as thin as human hair connected every clock in the room with the iron pole at its center.

Tone Hobart stood gazing at his handiwork, drinking in the sea of clattering sound that filled the room as grain fills a silo. He advanced slowly along the narrow path between the clocks, as if he were a pagan priest moving through ranks of worshipers gathered to bow before some leering ancient god.

He halted before the iron pole and studied the man who stood with his back to it. His wrists were bound behind his back with wire and the wire was attached to the iron pole, along with the thousands of strands drawn from as many thousands of clocks.

It was André.

He was alive.

He was disheveled, drenched with water, his skin abraded and smeared with the slime of the lake bottom. He raised his eyes to lock with those of Tone Hobart.

An icy gust of especial power swept through the skylight and behind Hobart the door of the workshop swung open and banged against its frame. Startled, Hobart turned his back on André and returned to the door. He peered into the hallway, then drew his head back into the room and slammed the door shut. This time he made sure that it was securely latched.

Kassia remained by the double doors, listening to the sounds of the clocks, and the sound of the wind. The volume of both grew, then diminished. The cycle was repeated, and the second time that the volume grew less, it remained so. She turned the handles on the doors, without haste and without hesitation.

From her position near the fireplace, Leonora crossed the room and stood facing Kassia.

She peered into the face of the other woman. "Where are you going?"

Kassia leaned her back against the double doors. "I am going to bury André."

Despite the events of the day, Leonora was not beyond shock. "How?"

Kassia tilted her head, indicating the far side of the parlor. "The fireplace tools," she exhaled. She raised her hands and held them between herself and Leonora. "And these."

"No!" Leonora's face was anguished. "I meant—how, when he isn't in the trunk?" Kassia frowned but Leonora went on. "I saw as I ran by. The trunk was open. He wasn't there!"

Kassia hissed dismissively. "You didn't want to see him, so he wasn't there." She pursed her mouth as would a teacher exasperated by a child's inability to grasp a wholly obvious lesson. "Such tricks hath strong imagination."

She slid past Leonora and crossed the room to stand before the fireplace. She handled the flat-bladed ash-shovel and the harpoon-like poker, studying and considering their utility. Leonora, wearied by helplessness and mystification, sank into the great chair that Tone Hobart had occupied. She focused her attention on the metallic dancer, shutting out the horror and despair of her situation.

Kassia's study of the fireplace tools was interrupted by Leonora's plaintive voice, calling her name. She turned and saw Leonora hunkered down in the chair, her elbows resting on one of its heavily-padded arms, her chin in her hands. She looked like a weary child seeking comfort from the warmth and odor of an absent parent trapped in a favorite piece of furniture.

Leonora touched the dancer's balance pole and set her to spinning in the firelight. She spoke, half to her companion and half to herself.

"My father could never have submitted to André's blackmail. There would have been a scandal. And he would have died of it. It would have finished off his heart, and he would have died."

Kassia offered a noncommittal, half-nod in response. "If only you hadn't given the letters to André," Leonora went on.

"That was the plan, my darling. You must have realized that by now. That was André's plan and my plan equally, from the outset. From that first day at the fashion show in London. Leonora, it was your father that it was all about."

Leonora seemed not to have heard Kassia's words. "Father will be safe from André now, won't he? His world will be safe." She sighed. Then, "Why do we always have to murder someone to make the world safe for someone else?" She stopped for a deep breath, then blurted, "I can't help you bury André."

Kassia held the fireplace tools in her arms, gazing down at the seated Leonora. The dark-haired Leonora seemed lost in contemplation of the metal figurine. Whenever the dancer slowed almost to a halt, Leonora would tap the weight at the end of her balance pole, and the dancer would twirl once more in the leaping firelight.

"Nobody ever helps a gravedigger," Kassia intoned. When it became obvious that Leonora was determined to study the dancing figurine rather than continue the conversation, Kassia crossed the parlor to the twin doors. She turned the handles, slipped out, and drew the doors shut behind her.

She stood in the foyer for a few seconds, her attention captured again by the clattering of clocks, then went to the main doorway and tried to open the door. The mechanism was heavy and stiff, as if it were used but infrequently, and surely not of late. As she struggled to work the mechanism, the fireplace tools tumbled from her arms and clattered onto the flagstone floor.

Before she could retrieve the shovel and poker a figure stepped from the shadow and bent to pick them up. Kassia stood transfixed as the man rose and held the tools toward her.

It was Tone Hobart. He had a barely perceptible smile on his lips. His great dark eyes beneath the broad brow and nearly-white hair seemed deep wells of darkness. He said nothing.

Kassia accepted the tools from Hobart. "No questions?" she asked.

Speaking softly, deliberately, he responded, "You are not the person to ask them of."

At last Kassia was able to work the mechanism that held the heavy front door shut. She stepped across the threshold, into the moist night of French springtime, and drew the door shut behind her.

Tone Hobart turned away, crossed the foyer to the double doors of the parlor, and let himself in. He stood for a time watching Leonora. The flames set off her dark hair and pale skin dramatically. She ignored Hobart, remaining transfixed by the dancing figurine.

The clattering of the clocks had entered the room with Hobart. Now he shut the twin doors behind himself, dampening down the sound to a fraction of its former volume. He crossed to stand over Leonora, seated in the great chair, studying the spinning dancer.

"Leonora?"

She raised her eyes to him.

"How did he die, Leonora?"

She smiled faintly and answered as matter-of-factly as if Hobart had asked the name of her favorite novel or the manufacturer of her wristwatch. "He was killed."

Hobart nodded. "How was he killed?"

"I never really cared for him," Leonora said. "He broke my father's heart, weakened it forever, and so I hated him."

Again, Tone Hobart asked, "How was he killed?"

Leonora held a long silence, as if she were remembering the events of her childhood, or the events of the past few hours. Hobart stood waiting, not so much with patience as with indifference. As if he had all the time in the world at his disposal, or as if time were both meaningless and valueless to him.

When Leonora finally answered Hobart's repeated question it was with a single word. "Quickly."

"By you and Kassia Paine?" Hobart asked.

"She told me what to do. She told me to find the Thanatos tree. I found it in the woods. I was to pick a single leaf. Thanatos means death, you know."

Hobart did not speak, so Leonora resumed.

"André told us the tree grows in lovely abundance in these parts. I obeyed Kassia and I found one without difficulty."

Tone Hobart waited patiently for her to continue. He had plenty of time.

"I'll never forget his face. He knew he'd drunk something fatal, yet he went on smiling, like a crushed clown."

Hobart's eyebrows rose. "A crushed clown?"

"When we were little, we had a clown doll. His head was hollow, made of plastic or hardened rubber, I don't know. It might even have been porcelain. It was so long ago, it's so hard to remember. But all it took was to ride over his face on a bicycle and his head was crushed. Beyond repair. I've always associated clowns and broken faces with death."

She raised her eyes to Hobart's. "My sister loved the clown."

"Your sister?" he asked gently. "Is Kassia your sister?"

Leonora smiled but flicked her eyes away from Hobart. "You might call us sisters. Perhaps more than sisters. It's not for me to say."

"But you have a sister? Or you did? A real sister?"

She looked at him again. "She couldn't bear to hurt my father. And me. She begged André to abandon his scheme, begged him. But he had those heartbreaking letters Daddy had written to Kassia, and he thought they would be negotiable."

"Then Kassia is not your sister."

"She's American. I'm English." She reached with one fingertip and set the metallic dancer to spinning again. "I did have an English sister, too, but she's dead now. As dead as a clown with a crushed head. But my father was very grateful when he saw what we'd done to the clown. He said, 'You've made my world safe for me.'"

Tone Hobart squatted beside the big chair. The dancer had slowed her spinning, had nearly stopped, and now it was he who set her in motion again. "How does one get a poison leaf into a blackmailer?" he asked Leonora.

"We put it in the shaker, and shook it. Kassia poured and I served and he drank."

Hobart nodded his understanding. He stood up and moved away from the chair. "I didn't think he'd drowned," he mused, "and I had to know."

Leonora looked up at him. "What did you say, Mr. Hobart?"

"I had to know if he'd died unnaturally." He rubbed his long chin with fine fingers. "I don't imagine it really matters. There can't be anything overly unnatural in a thing that causes so natural a phenomenon as death."

He saw that Leonora was gazing at him in bafflement. He smiled reassuringly. "I've intruded upon your reverie. Forgive me. I came in to see if you were comfortable."

"Mr. Hobart, why do you keep a useless clock?" She shot a glance at the broken clown-faced clock on the mantel.

Hobart said, "Why do you keep useless memories?"

"My mother had taken my sister and me to Brighton for the day, and she met a man on the boardwalk. My real sister, my English sister, not my American, well, not my American. The man wanted Mother's little girls to like him, so he threw some balls and won the clown for us. Like any prize won on a boardwalk, it was cheap and tawdry."

Not Kassia then? This was a story of Leonora and the other sister? The real sister. But which sister was real? Hobart wondered. There was no knowing.

"My mother ran off soon afterwards." Leonora gazed back through time at the saddening memory. "After she was gone my father could never bear to look at that clown."

Almost with regret, Hobart asked, "Would you be very unhappy if your murdered clown came suddenly back to life?"

"How could he?"

"All dead things were once alive."

"In the past," she amended.

"In the past," he agreed.

"But the past is gone."

"Is it?"

Abruptly, she turned away, her body shaken by an unexpected chill. He moved closer and knelt beside her chair, a small, shining enthusiasm in his eyes. The air of melancholy that had surrounded him was dispelled.

"Suppose the past and the present are two separate time cycles." He spoke rapidly, as if expressing for the first time a concept that had been pent in his mind for a very long time. "Suppose they coexist, coiling around us concurrently. Then all one need do is cause a slight tilt. Tilted one way, the present would slide into the past. Tilted the other way, the past would tumble into the present. And with it would come past things as they were before they died."

His face was close to hers, as close as a lover's to a lover's, but she felt only a small, cold terror rising like fine dust that had made its way into her windpipe.

"Yes, Miss Edmond." He was whispering now, but somehow his whisper seemed louder than his full-throated voice had been minutes ago.

"It can be done," he insisted. "It *has* been done. For one fraction of a fraction of a moment, the cycles were tilted. The past slid into the present. And I tumbled back to life."

His eyes glowed with an almost erotic fervor. "If I can make it happen again, Miss Edmond, and again and again . . . imagine the lost ones I can bring back, the great and the dear lost ones!"

He vaulted to his feet as startlingly as a painted Jack-in-the-box when an unsuspecting child opens its lid and releases the spring holding it in place. He reached and took her hand.

"I am going to show you my workshop! Where it happened! Where it may happen again!"

Frightened, she drew away from him, trying to sink back into the safety of the great chair. But he clutched her hand tightly, frowning at her, perplexed by her fearfulness.

"Don't you want him to be alive again?"

In a terrified whisper she managed a single syllable. "Who?"

"Your clown." He smiled softly at her. "André."

She shook her head, holding herself rigid, frightened.

"You're not a murderess, Miss Edmond," Hobart insisted. "If you were, you'd feel no guilt over the expedient removal of a clown and a blackmailer." He seemed to expand with anticipatory pride. "Come see him live again. The guilt will slip out of your heart."

He lifted her from the chair, using her two hands as levers; she, helpless to resist. Now, panic exploding, she ran toward the twin doors of the parlor, but he sped there as if he could move faster than time, arriving before she had covered the distance from the chair. He held one hand on the doors, preventing her from opening them, while he extended the other toward her in invitation.

The row of naked light bulbs hanging from the low ceiling of the corridor nearly brushed Tone Hobart's head as he led Leonora toward his workshop. She did not resist, but neither did she follow him willingly. Rather, she moved like a woman without will, setting one foot ahead of the other like a clockwork mannequin.

Hobart grasped the doorknob with one hand. As he opened the door there emerged from his workshop a deafening clamor of clattering clocks and a rushing whirlwind of wet air. The door responded to the pressure he exerted on it, swinging back on its timeworn hinges.

Leonora, behind him, stood with her hand over her mouth, too frightened either to advance or to flee, waiting to see what lay behind the door.

When she did, her frozen legs and frozen voice broke free. She uttered scream after piercing scream, then whirled like the metal dancer in the room downstairs and fled down the low hallway, dodging light bulbs as she scurried frantically away from the object of her terror.

Tone Hobart, unstartled by the prospect of his workshop and its contents, turned lazily to watch Leonora in her flight. He nodded but did not pursue.

But when he turned again, pushed the workshop door wide and observed all that was in the room, his calm was shattered. The mad spider's nest of hair-thin wires and clattering timepieces was undisturbed. The iron pole that stretched from the floor of the workshop to the opening in the roof and into the storm-driven night was intact.

But the water-soaked and mud-splattered man whose bound wrists had held him helplessly attached to the iron pole, was nowhere to be seen. All that remained of him was a path of footprints in water and mud, prints of naked feet, leading from the base of the iron pole to the door.

A gust of wind made Kassia's eyes tear as no emotion could, and threatened to pull her honey-blond hair from its carefully arranged chignon and set it snapping like a storm-blown cloth. She stood beside the Rolls, made her way to the trunk, and released the catch that held its lid in place.

Spring loaded, the lid flew upward with the suddenness of a Jack-in-the-box, but even before Kassia could look inside she was startled and her attention called away by a faint but distinct call. A voice was calling her name, Leonora's voice.

Kassia turned, trying to locate the source. It was more than a call. It was a desperate cry of terror. She moved toward the woods; the cry had seemed to come from them. She did not pause to look into the Rolls's trunk. She did not see André within, lying as she had left him hours before, drenched and mud-smeared on this wet and mud-covered road.

Where was Leonora?

Where had she gone?

Tone Hobart carried a woman's form through the wind-riven night, to the château. Before him, sightless Colas flung open the heavy door, then hurried past, as confident of his way as one fully sighted. He swung the parlor doors open and Hobart carried the limp form of Leonora Edmond inside.

Behind Hobart, Colas carefully closed the parlor doors, then advanced to stand near the others.

Leonora lay breathing softly on the sofa. The warmth of the fire on the hearth, the comfort of the cushioned sofa, the presence of Hobart with his reassuring strength and of Colas with his seemingly unconditional sympathy, all helped her to yield to her fatigue and exhaustion. She felt warm and drowsy.

She thought she heard the drone of the two men's voices, but could not understand their words.

The cart was so heavy that it took all her strength to push it. She wanted to stop and rest, but she knew that if she did, she would never be able to make the heavy wheels turn again. Not in the deep, cold mud that covered the surface of the road. Moaning with grief and fatigue, she pushed. The wagon hit a rut and threatened to overturn. If it did, the coffin would surely slide off.

Someone in the procession, she knew, carried the tools necessary for the job that had to be done. The fireplace tools were inadequate to the task of emptying, then filling, a grave, but they were all that she had.

A man's voice—Tone Hobart's voice—startled her like a splash of icy water.

"Miss Edmond? You said you poisoned him with a leaf of the Thanatos tree. Are you certain it killed him? Do you know that he truly died?"

Leonora peered left and right, seeking the source of the voice. Her stinging, tear-filled eyes saw only desolation. Still, she must reply.

"He truly died. And we are going to bury him. We will do it as we must. With fingernails and fireplace tools if we must."

Kassia whirled and brandished the fire-poker and flat-bladed shovel. "Your father wants to know why you're delaying the burial." She spoke in as harsh and demanding a tone as Hobart.

Leonora turned her head. Over her shoulder she saw a man following her. "I'm being followed, Daddy."

"Leonora?" The man was older than she, with white hair, an age-seamed face, and a distinguished bearing. He carried the doll that the bicycle wheel had crushed so many years before. "If anyone learns of this . . . if you didn't really kill him . . . the scandal will finish off my heart."

"We did, Daddy!" Leonora was desperate to convince him of the truth. "We killed him all dead. Daddy, how can I reassure you?"

Tone Hobart's disembodied voice spoke again. "How long had he been in the trunk when I found him?"

Leonora felt Kassia's hand on her arm. The hand that had—that she—Leonora strove to blink away the images of the things that hand had done. Kassia spoke: "Tell your father he was dead when I pulled him out of the water."

"Could he merely have been unconscious?" Tone Hobart's voice asked.

Leonora released the heavy wooden handles of the funerary cart and used her hands to wrest the broken clown doll from her father's grasp. She blinked once and saw Hobart and Colas standing over her in the château parlor. She returned willingly to darkness as their conversation continued.

"Could someone have dragged his body down the stairs and out of the house, Colas, without you or me having seen or heard?"

"It's been a noisy rain, Mr. Hobart."

"I saw Kassia Paine leave," Hobart said. "I remember I was sadly amused, imagining her wonder when she opened the empty trunk. I came in here, then. And I did not hear her return to fetch the body." He paused, then asked, "Was it you, Colas?"

"No. Nor did I."

"You didn't take the body away, Colas."

"No. I did not."

"He tumbled back, Colas. Just as I did!" Leonora heard Hobart's shuffling movements as he closed the distance between the two men. "I told you, Colas. I told you it was no accident. He was dead, and now he's alive. He's out there somewhere—alive!" He gave a small snort. "I'd better go and find him, and explain it all to him."

Leonora heard Hobart's hurrying footsteps, heard the twin doors open and then close again as he departed.

Tone Hobart moved purposefully across the foyer and drew open the heavy wooden door. Before he could step outside the château he found himself confronting the honey-haired Kassia. He froze in his tracks, staring, but she dodged past him to enter the château. He paused for a moment to consider his next move, then continued on his way.

Kassia retraced Hobart's steps to the parlor. She twisted the twin handles and entered the room. She observed Colas calmly tending the fire, building up its level with small bits of wood from the bin beside the hearth. Nearby, Leonora lay on one of the upholstered sofas. When she heard the sounds of Kassia's arrival, Leonora opened her eyes and pushed herself upright.

Ignoring the man tending the fire, Kassia stood over Leonora. "Did you scream my name?" she demanded.

Leonora replied with a question of her own. "Did you bury him, Kassia?"

Kassia persisted. "I heard you scream."

"Your fingernails are clean," Leonora observed.

Kassia whirled to face Colas. He remained with his back to the room, tending the fire. "I heard my friend scream for me," Kassia asserted. "Why did she scream?"

Colas straightened from his work. Deliberately, he turned to face Kassia. "If you would listen to an old, blind man," he said in his soothing, patient tones, "he would tell you to leave this house at once."

"Why?" Kassia demanded.

"You are in the midst of much madness."

"Not all madmen are dangerous."

"You cannot see the distinctions between the benign and the deadly. You are not blind."

"Is that why you are not afraid? Is that why *you* stay here?"

Calmly, Colas explained, "This is my house." He could not see the reaction on her face, but he might have known what it would be. In any case, he heard her surprised gasp. "You mistook me for a servant," he observed.

Perhaps he waited for some response from her, but none came, so he resumed. "There's so little visible difference between a host and a servant." He smiled. "Mr. Hobart has been my guest for almost a year. He stumbled upon my house in the dead of night, just as you did."

He nodded, recalling the event.

"He was in flight, just as you were. You, Miss, and your companion." He nodded toward Leonora's form, still on the sofa.

"A blind man's house is a good hiding place. And for a long time, Mr. Hobart's father could not find him. And then he found him. He'd come to take him back to America. You are from America, Miss, aren't you? I heard their bitter, loving arguments, and then I heard silence. I thought they'd both gone."

There was a moment of silence, and then the old man seemed to glare at Kassia; at least, one would have thought so, had Colas been sighted. Sternly, he said, "I must ask you to leave my house."

Kassia asked only, "At once?"

"Yes. At once."

Kassia looked at Leonora. The dark-haired young woman was sitting upright on the sofa, staring into some unseen distance, breathing quietly. Her eyes were open but whatever she was seeing, it was not the interior of the parlor.

"Where is Mr. Hobart?" Kassia asked.

Colas said, "Unless I've been wrong in my assessment of his madness, you need not fear Mr. Hobart."

Kassia drew a breath.

"It's the other one who is a danger to you," Colas resumed. "The one who drank your poisoned drink."

For the first time, Leonora entered the conversation. "I told them," she announced.

Kassia, appalled, whispered, "About André?"

"How could you tell anyone about André? How could anyone explain a man like André? A beast like André?" She shook her head, frowning. "No, all I did was tell them about our murdering André."

Furious, Kassia hissed, "Wouldn't it have been wiser not to?"

"I didn't intend to." Suddenly, balanced on a ticking second hand racing madly from defiance to contrition. "I didn't intend to. Somehow they pushed into my dream. They hovered over me. I couldn't move on until I had answered all of Mr. Hobart's questions."

Kassia turned away, her fury suddenly dissolving into weariness. She crossed to the second sofa and sat down on it. She fumbled for an ornate box that stood on a nearby table. It was of polished marble, with hinges of filigreed gold. She slipped a fingernail beneath the lid and opened the box, extracted a cigarette and put it to her lips.

Colas, hearing the box open and close, inferred what had taken place. He crossed to Kassia, removed a match from his jacket pocket, and held its flame until Kassia had lit her cigarette.

"It doesn't really matter," she offered, "Mr. Hobart is a poet, not a gendarme."

Opposing her companion, Leonora said, "Mr. Hobart is not a poet."

Kassia insisted, "He said he was."

Colas intervened. "A madman always thinks of himself as a poet. That's the solace that the devil provides, in return for what the madman gives the devil."

"Is he anything other than a madman?" Kassia asked.

Leonora replied, "Yes." She pushed herself fully upright and looked at her companion with newly clear eyes. "He has found a way to bring back the dead. As they were before they died."

Kassia turned toward Colas. He did not speak. The expression on his face was oddly like a gentle, wistful smile. What thoughts passed through his mind, only that tantalizing expression hinted.

"He has brought back André," Leonora continued, "as he was before we killed him."

Kassia shook her head. "André is dead, Leonora."

"Dead and buried?" Leonora asked.

Kassia did not reply. She had smiled, ever so faintly, when she spoke of André's death, but now the smile faded from her lips.

"He wasn't in the trunk, was he, Kassia?" Leonora rose from the sofa, her voice also rising until it was close to hysteria. "No! He wasn't! He got out! He's alive!"

His kindness asserting itself in his manner, blind Colas stepped forward. "Would you allow me to explain, Miss?"

Leonora ignored the offer. Her voice rose to a still shriller pitch. "André is alive! Again! I hear him walking around us, back and forth. I've been listening, and I've been hearing him. Listen—now!"

To Kassia, kind Colas said, "Ask her to hear me, Miss."

Kassia's voice was like a fist. "Leonora!"

But Leonora ignored the word. She commanded, "Listen!"

She crossed from the couch to a tall, heavily drape-covered window. She swept the thick, ancient material aside, revealing the old panes set in their leaded frames. The night outside was dark as the center of a thunder cloud, but for a fraction of a second, a sheet of glaring lightning turned it into a nightmare landscape of white forms and black shadows.

And the face.

The face at the window was that of Tone Hobart. He stood frozen while the flash illuminated his face; then, as it faded to darkness, he scurried away like a thief caught peering into the happy domicile of a normal family.

No one pursued Hobart. Instead, Leonora permitted the heavy drapes to fall back into position, covering the window and shutting the house off from the outside world and all its icy violence.

Colas made his way to the mantel and lifted down the decanter of brandy. He placed it carefully on the table, fetched snifters, and placed them beside the decanter. Perhaps oddly, he then straightened, leaving the squatty glasses empty and the decanter full.

Kassia stood now beside the fire. Leonora perched on the couch, as if uncertain whether to settle into its cushions or bolt from the room.

Colas, until now the man of the moment, the man of the present, had for once become the man of past time. He stood musing of bygone events, his sightless eyes fixed on images invisible to the others. To him—? Who could tell?

"I remember it as if I had seen it," he said. His soft, cultured voice had fallen to a low drone, yet every word was clearly audible. "He had screamed in his delirium."

Was the expression that played at the edges of his lips the faintest of smiles, or a mere tic brought on by the stress of recollection?

"I confess, my life had been so bleak and undirected, I was shamelessly happy to hear even a delirious scream. You see, I'd assumed his father had induced him to return to America, and the awful silent days convinced me he'd gone. But that was not what had happened."

Sightless, Colas's other senses told him where the two women were. He turned toward Kassia. "Perhaps your paths crossed in America. Since you both lived there, Miss Paine."

She shook her head, either forgetting or not caring that he could not see the gesture. "It's a very big country. Everybody there doesn't know everybody else."

"Of course not," he replied, apologetically. "I meant that as a small joke, you see."

He paused to draw a breath. "In fact, his father had given him up and gone, and he had remained. And now, why, I heard him scream. And I went to him."

"You mean Hobart, don't you? He's a madman," Kassia barked.

"Of course I mean Mr. Hobart. But he is not a madman, I assure you, Miss." He resumed telling his story. "He'd been hanging around here for almost a week, bound there in his magnetic wires. You've seen them, now. That was the term he applied to them. Magnetic wires."

Colas's dead eyes seemed alive. "He'd been in a comatose state, I suppose, for he'd made not a sound. Yes, for almost a week. Astonishing that he could survive that long, without nourishment or water. But when he screamed, I went up there to the room he calls his workshop. I unfastened him, and carried him to his bed, and brought him back to health."

He paused to lift the decanter and a second snifter, and pour brandy into the glass, and carry it to Kassia. She accepted the snifter, but did not imbibe of the liquor. She asked Colas, "And he thought you'd brought him back to life?"

"No. Not I. He believed his time-shifting device had done it. He has spent a great deal of time developing his theories of planes of time, and tilting those planes, and of persons and events shifting from present to past and from past to present."

"Sheer insanity!"

"Perhaps not. Who is to say?" The ghostly smile came and went. "Perhaps if we tilted in another direction we could slide into the future, and see the marvels that lie in the days of our distant descendants. Assuming that we do not destroy the world before their day arrives."

Colas raised his shoulders in a gentle shrug. "Regarding Mr. Hobart, well, he still believes he was dead, and that his machine rescued him from the grip of death. He will not give up the belief that he was dead during those comatose days, and that the cycles of time tilted and slid him out of the dead past and into the lively present."

He bent to raise the decanter and fill the second snifter for Leonora. He offered it to her, but she appeared unaware of the gesture, remaining perched as she had been on the edge of the sofa.

Kassia, observing this bit of by-play, lowered her own glass, crossed to take the snifter from Colas and held it close to Leonora's face. At first there was no reaction. Then, as the fumes of the warming liquor reached Leonora's nostrils, they twitched. Her tongue darted out, as would that of a viper testing the air for the vibration of enemy or prey.

She stirred, raised her eyes to Kassia's, then took the glass in both her hands. She drank the brandy with surprising quickness. She stood, a startled expression on her face, like a sleeper when a loud alarm has sounded.

She asked, "When did the rain stop?"

Colas answered, "Almost the moment you came in out of it." He turned his sightless eyes toward the curtained window, as if neither his blindness nor the opacity of the heavy cloth could keep him from seeing into the night beyond. "You can go now," he added. Then, raising his voice in ambiguity, in question or in request, "Quickly?"

Leonora responded. "Yes, quickly. Thank you for your kindness. And your rationality." She turned toward her companion. "Kassia?"

"Please, let's stay here, Leonora. Just till morning. I'll be finished by then."

"No." When Leonora exhibited one of her rare outbursts of determination, the usually dominant Kassia did not press her point. "We'll go now, as we've been asked to do," Leonora continued.

Kassia nodded and walked to the twin doors. She opened them. Leonora passed into the foyer, followed by Kassia, who closed the doors behind her.

But once they were out of the parlor and out of the presence of Colas, the women seemed to resume their more customary dynamic. Standing in the foyer, deluged again in the sea of mechanical clattering, Kassia leaned her back against the twin parlor doors. Leonora turned back to face her.

"You can wait in the car," Kassia offered, "while I bury him."

Leonora whispered. "Did he die, Kassia?"

"Mr. Hobart?"

A tiny shake of her dark-tressed head. "Not Hobart, Kassia. Did André die?"

Kassia strode past Leonora, swung open the heavy front door of the château, and stood gazing into the night. The light from the château illuminated the Rolls, which stood now close to the door of the château.

Even as Kassia remained gazing in horror, Leonora behind her craning for a view, the trunk lid swung up.

It had been pushed from the inside, and now André could be seen, kneeling within, pushing himself to his feet and climbing from the trunk. He was fully clothed, in the slacks, shirt, blazer, and sandals that had been placed in the trunk with him when the Rolls had stood near the dark lake.

In his hand he held an empty martini glass.

He offered his most beautiful smile.

André's sandals hit the graveled surface of the driveway with a soft sound. He caught himself, maintaining his balance with the perfect ease of the athlete not yet gone to seed. His smile became, if anything, even broader. He thrust the empty glass toward Kassia.

"Refill, please!"

Leonora and Kassia had stood like pillars of frozen shock during André's astonishing performance, but the sound of his voice freed them from their paralysis.

First Leonora turned away and ran back, through the foyer and up the stairs within the château.

André laughed and started after her, then thought better of it and halted. Instead, he turned and gazed at Kassia. She backed slowly away from him.

Leonora scrambled frantically up the stairs. When she reached their summit she raced down the bright corridor with its row of low-hanging bare electric bulbs. She passed closed and darkened doorways, doorways she had seen before but ignored. This time, too, she hurried past them, only to bring up short outside Tone Hobart's workshop, the playroom of a demented clock-maker.

The door stood open, and the dazzling light that sprang from the workshop was outdone in its violent assault on the senses only by the insane clattering of Hobart's clockwork masterpiece. It seemed impossible that the din could exceed its previous levels, but such must surely be the case.

Leonora halted, spun, and retraced her footsteps. She dared not make her way down the stairs. Instead, out of the darkened and closed doors that lined the hallway, she chose one at random, her heart beating in her chest like a wild metronome.

She tried the door handle and exhaled in relief, realizing only then that she had been holding her breath in terror and suspense. She shoved the door open and plunged into darkness.

Lightning flared outside the château, and illuminated the tiny room through a single tall window. There was nothing in the room save the wild rushing of cold, moist air, and—

And—

Leonora screamed.

"Daddy!"

A blackened, rough-hewn timber ran from side to side in the room. Whether it served a structural purpose or merely one of decoration, was not clear.

What was clear was the visage of the man who hung from the timber. He wore the morning suit of a London banker, a dark homburg on his head, a metal-ferruled, furled umbrella under one arm. His head was tilted at a quizzical angle.

He hung from the timber by one strong arm. At his feet his attaché case had fallen open to reveal a clown doll with a broken face.

Leonora shrieked.

Sightless Colas wandered through the woods beyond the château. Seemingly as familiar with the paths and perils of the forest as he was with the corridors and quarters of the house, he called with growing anxiety, "Mr. Hobart! Mr. Hobart! Mr. Hobart!"

Colas reached a fork in the path and decided, almost at random, which direction to take. The wood was ancient. It had been traversed, long ago, by animals' trails that in turn became hunters' trails, then rutted cart tracks, and had finally become broad and flat enough to permit the passage of a motor car. In the darkness of the night and the wood, Colas's sightlessness hardly mattered. He called again, "Mr. Hobart!"

Yet the night's storm was not without its effect. An ancient tree, weak with the years and brittle with dry rot, had been uprooted. Its trajectory had carried it into a clearing, and a limb reached across Colas's path like an adolescent trickster.

Colas's toe caught beneath the limb. He pitched forward, hands out-held to break his fall.

Instead, they encountered another pair of hands. They belonged to a man seated on the wet earth.

These hands steadied Colas and helped him up, helped him to regain his balance. He stood, panting with relief, his face wet with precipitation and with perspiration.

Tone Hobart asked, "Are you all right now, Colas?"

"Yes, thank you, I'm unhurt, Mr. Hobart. He said you'd been run down by his car. Are you hurt?"

"No. I merely fell aside as he sped away. I was trying to explain how he had been dead, and how I had brought him back to life. He was amused, but not terribly interested. He said he was itching to find his young ladies. He thanked me for giving him a nonsense with which to tease them."

Calm now, Colas resumed his customary mien. "The rain is dirty, Mr. Hobart. Let me help you to the house."

"That kind of man is best left in the past, Colas, in the dead, harmless quiet of the past." He shook his head, an expression of bitter disillusionment marking his features. "I am sorry I brought him back. I was wrong to bring him back."

Softly, compassion filling his voice, Colas replied. "You couldn't have known he was a thing of such evil. Do you know the line, Mr. Hobart? 'Imagination bodies forth the forms of things unknown.'"

Tone Hobart, still seated on the wet earth, said, "Help me up, Colas. I'm going to undo what my blindness has done. I'm going to go and kill him."

Was it indifference to life and death? Was it the gambler's thrill at placing the ultimate bet against incalculable odds? Or was it merely the arrogant demonstration of dominance and of supreme confidence?

Whatever his motivating force, André sat on the sofa, smiling serenely. Perhaps it was none of these motivations. Perhaps it was sublime ignorance: ignorance of the presence of Kassia, standing behind the sofa, an iron object in her hands. She had abandoned the flat-bladed fireplace shovel—absurd instrument with which to dig a grave long enough and deep enough to hold this man—and stood with the heavy, sharply-pointed poker poised to deliver sudden, angry death.

She raised the poker overhead, then lowered it again, circled the sofa and stood facing André.

He gazed up at her neither in anger nor in fear nor in shock. He appeared to be merely bemused. He patted the cushion beside his leg.

She sank to the sofa and softly kissed him on the cheek.

He put his arms around her, drew her close, and kissed her on the mouth. He moved his lips tenderly from her own lips to her ear. A wisp of honey-blond hair escaped from its place as if it had a will of its own and wished to play the miniature coquette.

André asked, "What did you put in my drink, Kassia?" His voice was the tender whisper of passion.

"A leaf," she replied.

"Of the Thanatos tree?"

"Yes."

He grinned with merry pleasure. "No wonder it killed me."

Kassia drew her face away from André's. Her grin was not the same as André's. "She must have pulled it off the wrong tree," she ventured. Then she moved away from him.

The two of them moved around each other, André and Kassia, Kassia and André, like matador and bull, each studying the other, each patiently waiting for the opportunity to advance *con espada o cuerno,* with sword or horn, to deliver the killing cut.

"Why did you want to kill me, Kassia?" André lunged. "Wasn't ours a beautiful love affair?"

"Yes," she parried. And riposted, "Until it became a conspiracy."

"Sooner or later every love affair becomes a conspiracy."

"I had decided I didn't want to hurt Leonora's father after all. Those two are touching. So decent. And they had the artless courage—or foolhardiness—to become my friends."

André shook his head with the weary resignation of one exasperated by a slow-witted child's failure to comprehend. "But I brought you together for the sole purpose of hurting them. In the pocketbook, of course. Where it hurts the most. Surely you remember the hours we spent planning this crime, between the other pleasures of our dalliance."

In a flash, Kassia abandoned her sardonic mantle and returned to the nakedness of straightforward expression. "We are not going to destroy him, André."

"He destroyed himself." Surprised and impressed by Kassia's lapse into or aspiration to directness, André touched her shoulder with the tip of one finger. "You're a sleek sack of sin, Kassia. Men like Leonora's father should never write letters to girls like you. It's self-destructive. And self-destruction is a luxury which no man should be permitted to enjoy free of charge."

Kassia looked at him with disgust. "Why didn't you die?"

"I did," he replied simply.

He smiled then, or his lips moved in the beginning of a smile but stopped somewhere along the way. His eyes gleamed with some small shock, some look of unexpected confusion. He drew his hand away from Kassia's shoulder and placed both hands on his stomach. He seemed surprised to find it just where it belonged.

Kassia observed, the expression in her eyes unreadable.

André blinked. "Find Leonora, Kassia! We must hurry." He drew a series of breaths, each one more desperate and uncertain than the one before. Pausing for a fraction of a beat between each pair of words, he gasped, "Maybe there is a Thanatos tree."

He closed his eyes, Kassia watching all the while. He squeezed his eyes shut, as if they could be more closed than closed. He looked like a small boy experiencing the anguish of great pain for the first time, his expression speaking of shock as much as it did discomfort.

Then, as suddenly as it had appeared, the expression of pain on his face was gone. He drew himself to his full height, fixed his gaze on Kassia, his expression the old cruel smile. He stood over Kassia and held her with his eyes until she had to turn away.

He said, "It's spring in England, Kassia. It doesn't last long there. Let's not miss a juicy-rich minute of it."

"André." Kassia's whisper carried a plea. "You have such riches. So many have given you so much. You don't need an old man's wealth."

He replied, "I have planes and boats and villas and jewels, all the cacophonies with which beggar boys drown out the groan of insecurity. I am rich, but I am noisy rich, Kassia. And I want to be quiet rich."

She shook her head at his revelation of a weakness of which he was ashamed. She smiled inwardly. Thrust, parry, riposte. "You have to be heir to that, André. You can't be born in the sewers of a noisy world and grow up to be anything other than a noisy, sewer-minded man."

André smiled outwardly. "You've pierced the heart of my psychic disorder. Now we truly must go."

He leaned down and kissed the honey-gold top of her head. Gently but firmly he removed the poker from her hand. He took a few steps away from her, swinging the poker experimentally as if testing the weight and balance of a riding crop before setting out to master a beautiful but high-spirited horse.

At the double doors of the parlor he stood, holding the doors open, the poker still in his grasp. He called, "Leonora," and when there was no response in a brief moment, again, "Leonora!"

No voice replied, no sign was given that he had been heard. But the foyer was filled with the terrible ticking of the uncounted timepieces in Tone Hobart's workshop.

From the parlor behind André came Kassia's voice. "Perhaps she died."

Without turning back to look at Kassia, André smiled again, glancing toward the outside door at the opposite side of the foyer. "Then our time-slanting host will simply have to tilt her a little slant and slide her back to us."

Perhaps André had timed the incident or perhaps the controlling hand was that of fortune. But even as André spoke, blind Colas drew back the front door.

Tone Hobart stood upon the threshold, then stepped deliberately forward, onto the flagstone flooring. He stared in silence at André, who returned his gaze in echoing silence.

Colas spoke low to Hobart, so André could not hear. "Please, Mr. Hobart. There is poetry in madness, but nothing rhymes in murder."

Hobart stared at Colas, bafflement written on his features. After a moment he strode past Colas, past André. Moving like an automaton, André abandoned his post and followed behind. They crossed the foyer to the still-opened doors of the parlor. They stepped into the parlor, the doors standing open behind André, while beyond, in the foyer, Colas remained, his ears and perhaps some other, more subtle organs of sensation, serving in lieu of his eyes.

Standing in the doorway, the poker in his one hand while he tapped its shaft across the open palm of the other, André now ignored Kassia, directing his full attention, instead, to Tone Hobart.

Hobart crossed to the polished wood table beside the great chair, the table where the metal dancer stood on tiptoe on her platform, her balancing pole in her hands. For once she was motionless. Hobart slid open a drawer in the table and withdrew a small revolver. It was of flat black metal with blackened wooden grips. Its barrel was short and it would in all likelihood be inaccurate at any great distance, but it was surely an adequate weapon for use in the mortally close quarters of this ancient room.

He took note of Kassia's presence, even if André had not. He smiled at her, a brief smile, small and sad. He turned back and spoke past André, to Colas standing yet in the foyer near the parlor doors.

"Close the doors, Colas. And lock them from without. Please."

Another of the infinite variety of smiles on his lips, André moved away from the doors, so that he would not interfere with Colas's movement. The doors closed with the thump of old, heavy wood and the click of well-oiled metal.

Tone Hobart lowered himself into the great chair, the black revolver in his lap, one hand holding it with an easy familiarity. With his free hand he gave the dancer's balance pole a gentle shove. She swirled and swirled, reflecting the firelight in dazzling flashes.

He gazed at the dancer for a moment, then tore his eyes away from her and fixed them on André. "I am sorry I brought you back. I was wrong to bring you back."

"Back from where?" André laughed.

"Hell, I imagine. It's where you belong. Isn't it where you were? Don't you remember it?"

André ignored the questions; instead of answering them asked one of his own. "Do you intend to right your wrong?"

"Yes."

"With that?" He nodded, indicating the gun in Hobart's lap.

"No." Hobart shook his head. "With this—" he gestured ever-so-slightly with the revolver "—I shall persuade you to return to my workshop."

"It may not be loaded. For all I know the revolver is empty. Or loaded with blanks. Perhaps the ammunition is so old it won't fire any more. Or . . . perhaps you are too cowardly to pull the trigger."

"Good questions, every one. You can get your answers easily enough. Simply refuse to obey me."

"I shall hold my questions, then, for some other time."

Directing his words to Kassia, Hobart said, "I'll try to slant the cycles the other way. I'll try to send him back into the past." To André he said, "I believe Hell will be glad to take you back. I don't know how many are privileged to visit those quarters, and leave, and return there again, but that will be your fate. You're clearly one of Hell's own."

There was silence, and then André burst into laughter. He lifted the poker like a hunter's javelin, and hurled it with surprising force and accuracy into the fireplace. It struck with a tone like the hourly sounding of a great clock's chime. He rolled away from the doors, whirling around the parlor like the dancer swirling on her platform.

His laughter ceased with shocking suddenness, replaced by a spasm of pain. He clutched his stomach, staggered to the sofa and fell onto it, his knees snapping against his chest with a thump as he collapsed into fetal position.

He uttered a single, low cry, and then was silent and motionless.

And then, with astonishing swiftness, the attack ended, leaving him intact and alive and seemingly unharmed. He blinked and looked at Hobart and at Kassia, as surprised, perhaps, as they were by his peculiar behavior.

To Hobart he said, "Do you know what a madman you are?"

Kassia whispered his name, "André!" It was an appalled exclamation.

"I detest the blitheness of madmen." André spat the words. "Why are they so fortunate? Why don't *they* hurt the way the incurably sane hurt? Why doesn't reality twist *their* vitals?"

As he spoke he rose carefully from the sofa and began walking slowly toward Tone Hobart. The latter had turned his face away from André, perhaps confident in his own armed strength, perhaps morally certain that André would obey his commands, or at the very least would remain unmoving, recalcitrant, willing to debate if not to comply.

Hobart's attention was fixed once again on the dancing figurine.

André spoke as if Hobart were unarmed, also. As if he himself was not in peril of his life, but was merely debating with an equal whom he regarded with a strange mixture of loathing and respect.

"Who are you, madman, that everyone should be so willing to humor you? You're not a curly-headed child, your delusions are not games. Your 'workshop' is not a nursery, it's a fool's cluttered madhouse, a trash-heap of clocks, a cobweb of common household wire."

He shook his head angrily.

"You stole me out of the warm little trunk of my car and you propped me against a cold, useless pole. And you truly believe such solemn silliness actually brought me back from the dead?"

He paused, and only the distant ticking of clocks was heard in the room; the ticking of clocks, and the crackling of flames, and the soft breathing of André and Hobart and Kassia.

"I was not dead. I was never dead. And there is no Thanatos tree. I spun them a tale of death, my two adoring sweethearts, and they believed it. Do you think I would allow myself to die at the hands of such inept, fancy murderers?"

His grin showed two rows of perfect, gleaming, hungry teeth.

"But, oh! The fun of pretending! It tickled me to the pit of my soul to peep through my lashes and watch them shiver with guilt. It tickled me! Just as it tickles me to break your hold on unreality."

During all of André's long monologue, Tone Hobart had not looked at him. Even when André stood over him, the spinning dancer held Hobart's gaze, not the other man. Now André reached for the black revolver that lay in Hobart's lax grip, across his lap.

He lifted the revolver; Hobart did not resist. André asked, "Shall I do you this one small favor?"

He raised the revolver and held it at waist level, carefully aimed and blew a hole in the great chair, a fraction of an inch from Tone Hobart's head. Kassia's scream mingled with the echo of exploding gunpowder, bouncing off flagstone floor and masonry walls. Hobart's attention remained fixed on the dancer.

The twin doors flew open to reveal Colas, for once baffled by the event of the moment, his face a mask of anguish.

André backed away from Hobart and the damaged chair and threw the smoking revolver across the room. It crashed to the floor and skittered to a halt at Kassia's feet.

She bent and lifted it by its grip. She raced toward the great chair. Upon her arrival, André reached for her, grasped her by the arm and pulled her face close to his own. He began to sing:

London Bridge is falling down,
Falling down, Falling down,
And we cannot wait for Leonora!

He spun Kassia around and shoved her ahead of him, toward the open twin doors, past Colas, into the long foyer. Although Kassia held the short-barreled revolver, neither she nor André seemed to pay it heed. André was the active member of the process; Kassia was acted upon.

At the heavy front door of the château André reached past Kassia and seized the ornate handle that worked the mechanism. He swung the door back and shoved her ahead of him once more, into the cold wet air of the French spring night.

Within seconds the engine of the huge Rolls had roared into life and the car had pulled out of the driveway, distancing itself from the château, disappearing into the French countryside.

Within the château, Colas crossed the parlor to the chair and laid his hand on Hobart's face, ascertaining that he was alive and unharmed.

"The rain is dirty, Colas," Hobart murmured, "will you please close the door?"

Colas nodded in satisfaction and assent, went to the front door and closed it, then returned to the parlor, leaving the twin doors open.

Hobart looked up at the blind Colas, Hobart's eyes deeper and more thoughtful than ever. "Colas?" he asked melancholically, "Colas, please tell me the truth. Have you simply humored me?"

Was Colas being kind, or merely evasive—or did his answer qualify as both? "I know what it is to be blind."

Tone Hobart would not be put off with an evasion, however well it was intended. "When you found me up there, I had been dead for a while. Do you not believe that?"

"There is death and there is death." Slippery Colas.

"Can you dare to be even reasonably certain that my device is a 'trash heap'?"

"I prefer it not to be."

"Why, Colas?"

The old man expounded, "Lovers and madmen have such seething brains, such shaping fantasies, that apprehend more than cool reason ever comprehends."

"So many loved people have died, Colas." Hobart, not particularly combative to start with, turned morbidly philosophical—or philosophically morbid. "So many loved people have died, Colas. In my time, and before my time. And to me it seemed all these endings were untimely. I wondered what would become of all the love left over. And so, with trash-heaps and cobwebs, I built an antidote...."

He paused, looking into Colas's blind eyes, seeking something there, something not easy to place a label upon. "... and I allowed my antidote to resurrect an evil clown. No," Hobart hissed, "I am not the man to tinker with time. No man is that man. That man is God."

He extended his hand. "Good-bye, Colas."

"Where are you going, Mr. Hobart?" the sightless man asked mildly.

"I'm going back. Into the past. The dead, harmless quiet of the past."

Colas extended his own hand, unerringly despite his blindness. He took Hobart's hand in his own, held it briefly, then released it.

Hobart said, "I thank God that kindness is blind." He turned away from the old man and headed toward the double doors. He made his way upstairs, heading toward his workshop, toward his miraculous time machine, perhaps toward his personal elaborate trash-heap.

As he moved along the narrow hallway, dodging naked light bulbs, he passed an open doorway. He stopped and peered inside. These doors were never open; he didn't even know what lay behind them. He had never asked and Colas had never seen fit to volunteer the information.

Leonora's eyes were closed, her head had fallen onto her chest. For a fleeting instant Hobart wondered if she were dead, but he stood watching until he detected the slow, gentle rising and falling of her breast with each inhalation and exhalation. With that almost extrasensory sensitivity that tells us when we are being watched, Leonora awakened, blinking, shook her head in startlement, gazed up at Hobart.

She gave a tiny cry.

He smiled reassuringly. He saw that she held a sheet of folded paper—an old letter. He indicated the paper with a dip of his head.

"Did you read it?"

She glanced down at the letter, as if surprised to find it in her hand. She shook her head from side to side. No, she had not read the letter.

Hobart reached for it. When she declined to snatch it away from his outstretched hand, he took it gently from her. He said, "I wrote this, you know."

She did not reply.

"I wrote it when I was very young," he reiterated. He must have remembered it vividly, for he was able to recite its contents without even glancing at the page.

"It reads, 'Dearest Father,'" he said. "It reads, 'Do not be angry with me for killing the cat. I was experimenting with a way to bring dead people back to life. I want to bring Mother back. Your loving son, Tone.'"

Leonora had held her eyes locked on his face as he recited the text of this ancient communication. Now that he was finished she turned her face away, an anguished combination of emotions playing across her features. There was compassion for the agony of the long-ago boy who had written the letter, and the here-and-now man who could recite it from memory, and there was naked, rising fear at what this man, perhaps now a madman, intended to do to her.

A desperate pounding echoed through the château.

Colas left the parlor and hurried to the front door. He stood before it, not yet moving to open it. He called out, "Who is there?"

The voice that answered was anguished, breathless, barely coherent. Phrases tumbled, interspersed with pauses marked by ragged gasps. But the voice was clearly recognizable as belonging to Kassia:

"I jumped. From the car. And he tried. To run over me. And he crashed. Against a tree. And he stopped crying."

Colas worked the old latching mechanism and pulled the door open. Outside, standing at the head of the pathway that led to the door, Kassia continued her breathless speech.

"Please. Come. Make him. Cry again."

Colas nodded. Calm as ever, yet he managed to move with speed when he needed to. He slipped out of the château, holding his hand before him so that Kassia might take it, prepared to follow where she led.

In the darkened room where Leonora had fled rather than re-enter Tone Hobart's time-maddened workshop, Leonora crouched on the floor, her shoulders hunched like a frightened child's, her face averted from the world.

Hobart stood over her, gesturing as he tried to explain himself and his ill-starred efforts.

"My young intelligence had been stampeded by grief. I should have perceived then, by his anger, that it is morally wrong to fumble with fixed and lovely laws."

Leonora turned to watch Hobart's face. Her eyes indicated understanding. She nodded sympathetically.

Suddenly, Hobart fell to his knees. He took Leonora's face in his hands, holding his palms against her cheeks, gazing into her eyes. A dark, solemn softness informing his voice, he pled.

"Will *you* forgive me, Leonora?" He tilted his head as if a fresh idea had popped into his mind. "Someone here has to, in case no one there will."

Leonora rose carefully to her feet, Hobart matching her movements. They stood face to face, like lovers, holding each other hand to hand, too shy for more intimate embrace. They circled slowly, like dancers performing some antique gavotte.

When Leonora sensed that her back was to the door, she freed her hands from Hobart's and began to back away from him, slowly, moving toward the hallway.

He cried out, "Don't go! Stay! Please! I need you!"

She continued to edge away from him, and he tottered forward, step by tiny step, maintaining their proximity without contact.

"Someone will have to break those cobwebs." It was as if he had become, suddenly, the voice of clear, sweet reason. "And someone will have to smash those clocks. Dangerous dreams should not be left lying around. No, not once the dreamer has gone."

He extended one hand, came within a finger's width of touching her arm. But she spun away from him and leaped across the threshold of the room as if it were the bed of a shallow, icy stream. In the hallway she turned and ran toward the stairs—only to halt dead in her tracks.

At the stairway end of the hallway, her face and body illuminated to the pallid whiteness of a corpse, Kassia stood. She was striped with mud, covered with filth, soaked with rainwater. One shoe was missing. Her once snowy linen sheath was shredded. A long, slender streak of blood ran the length of her face, slashing in crimson anger from her temple to her jawbone.

But at the sight of Leonora her eyes went wide with happy relief. She spoke with the factual directness of a courier announcing the outcome of a distant battle.

"He is dead, Leonora. André is dead. All that evil is finally dead."

Leonora stood staring at Kassia. Thoughts swirled through her mind, emotions and recollections racing one after the other until she feared for her own grip on reality. Her mouth dropped open. To speak? To scream?

No word, no piercing cry emerged.

She felt the touch of a hand on her arm and bolted, leaving Tone Hobart in the hallway with Kassia.

Leonora ran toward Hobart's mad workshop. Behind her she heard the sound of his feet pounding down the hallway, thumping with each stride like the strokes of a massive metronome. She reached the workshop three strides ahead of him, leaped the threshold once more as if crossing a swift-flowing stream, as if she were fleeing from a vampire who could never, she knew, cross that icy running water.

She slammed the door in his face and struggled to fix the lock only to find that she could not do so without a key. She heard him pleading, pounding on the door, sobbing, "No! No, Leonora! No, not yet!"

She put her back to the door, steadied her feet on the floor, leaned against the heavy wooden door to keep it closed. All around her clock faces leered, movements ticked, pendulums swung, the mad clatter of the passing moments pounded at her eardrums.

And there was a pounding at the door as well, and after a moment, with one heavy impact, she felt herself thrown across the room, crashing into a web-work of fine wires, tumbling and bringing down the countless clocks hurtling and clashing as they landed on the flagstone, glass covers and metal hands and gears and springs and tiny screws and mysterious parts flying through the air, landing and bouncing like hailstones.

She saw Tone Hobart standing in the doorway, then advancing into the room, horror in his eyes, horror and the ineffable grief of a parent whose sole and beloved child lies mortally damaged before him.

"Don't hurt it," he begged, "I need it. Don't!"

He reached to pull her away from the tangled mechanism but she screamed and twisted away from him.

Kassia stood in the doorway, a strange smile on her lips, a strange expression in her eyes, freezingly cold and yet burning with a fury of its own, like a slab of dry ice clutched to one's naked bosom. She held the small black revolver in one hand.

She raised the revolver and held it at shoulder level, pointing it straight ahead, sighting carefully along its barrel. One would have thought her a trained and experienced markswoman. One might have been right.

She squeezed the trigger with deliberation, and when the weapon discharged the sound of its firing echoed off the stone flooring and masonry walls of the château until it sounded like the explosion of thunder.

A small red spot appeared on the back of Tone Hobart's garment.

He turned away from Leonora as if surprised, more as if his curiosity had been piqued than as if he had been mortally wounded. He turned slowly to see who had shot him. He recognized Kassia, nodded pleasantly to her as if she had performed some small favor at his request, and then fell backwards against the iron pole that ran from the workshop's floor to the opening in the roof and into the night.

He was supported upright, briefly, by the pole. Then he slid slowly to the floor, assumed a sitting position, then toppled over and lay unmoving. The blood pumped at first from his wound, then trickled, and finally ceased to flow.

From the hallway, Colas entered the workshop. Unseeingly but unerringly he crossed the room to the iron pole, knelt beside Tone Hobart's body and brushed his palm gently across Hobart's fine hair.

Kassia had lowered the revolver. It hung from the fingers of her hand, a thin wisp of smoke rising from its muzzle.

"Leonora?" Kassia's voice was a whisper.

Leonora struggled to untangle herself from the maze of wires that held her like a fly in a spider's web. She halted for a moment to give her attention to Kassia.

Kassia continued, still speaking in the breathless fragments of her terrified appearance at the château. "Ask the blind man. If he'll show us the way. To where we must go."

Leonora looked away from Kassia, looked instead to Colas. He seemed to sense her focus on him. He stood before her, once more the gracious, understanding host, once more the patient, helpful elder whose mannered diffidence made him seem almost like a servant.

The ticking of the surviving clocks, those which had not been smashed by Leonora's hurtling body when Hobart managed to force the workshop door open, continued, filling the workshop and the château and the springtime.

He waited for her to speak.

When the butler, Malachi, announced the arrival of the Misses Paine and Edmond, Tim Edmond all but flew down the staircase and across the vestibule of his Surrey house to greet them. He threw his arms around his daughter, then held her a few inches away from himself to gaze into her face. When he saw the tears there he fumbled for a pocket handkerchief and dried them for her. She took the handkerchief and smiled up at him as she had as a child and hugged him again, giggling and sobbing at the same time.

Only when Leonora was calmed and able to stand away from her father without lapsing into another emotional outburst, did Timothy Edmond turn to Kassia.

She moved toward him but before she could touch him he reached forward and took her hand in a formal greeting. "You're looking well, Kassia," he told her.

"I'd hoped—" She had started to say something, but the look on his face discouraged her from going on.

Instead, Tim Edmond said, "Come into the sitting room. When I heard you were at the airport I was prepared to come there to see you, but you would have none of it, so here you are. You left the Rolls in Paris, did you? No matter, that will be taken care of one way or another."

He had no need to show his daughter and her friend the way. They settled quickly into old furniture that had stood on old rugs for decades. The room was lined with bookcases of polished wood, filled with volumes dating from the seventeenth century to the latest memoirs and biographies.

Tall and dignified, Malachi entered the room silently carrying a large silver tray with coffee, tea, and small snacks.

"So you had a run-in with old Colas, did you?" Edmond asked.

The women both nodded.

"Quite a fellow, I should say. How is he doing?"

Kassia said, "I didn't know you knew him, Tim. You never mentioned him to me."

Edmond frowned. "There are many things you don't know, Kassia. You'll do better in life if you remember that." He nodded to the butler who poured tea for Timothy Edmond and his daughter Leonora, coffee for the American Kassia. Clearly, Malachi knew the two women and knew the tastes of all.

When he had finished, he withdrew.

A fire blazed on a hearth of tile and bricks. There was little other resemblance to the parlor of Colas's château.

"I knew Colas many years ago, neither at his home nor at mine. He had his eyes then. I was with him when he lost his sight. Blindness changed him for the better."

Leonora had lifted her cup and saucer. Suddenly the cup rattled and some droplets of tea leaped from it. She managed to lower the cup and saucer to the table without spilling more. She said, "Father, I saw you in France."

Timothy Edmond's eyebrows rose. "Did you. And how was that, daughter?"

"You were—Father, you were hanging."

"By the neck until dead, I suppose." He offered her a very peculiar smile.

"No. You were hanging—like a monkey from a beam. And you'd brought the broken doll. You remember the old broken doll with the clown face? It lay at your feet. I was so frightened, Father, I didn't understand. I still don't."

"It was a dream, Leonora. Don't let it bother you. I was in your dream, and you were in mine. That's all. I'll venture you saw a funeral procession on the road near Colas's château, as well."

She began to tremble. "How did you know that?"

"I saw the same procession, decades ago. Think of it as an oddity, an anomaly as Colas would say. As a warning perhaps. The ghost of losses past, don't you think? The ghost of losses yet to come? You know, there are those who think of ghosts as revenants of bygone events. But perhaps they are foreshadowings of the future." He shrugged his elegantly clad shoulders. "It's best to leave such things to themselves, I think, and tend to our own affairs."

He raised his eyes, contemplating a gilt-framed landscape on the opposite wall. "I suppose the greengrocer in Aix-Les-Bains still brings out supplies to Colas every week. Your mother and I spent a year at the château, you know. Before you were born, Leonora. A full year. Before you or your sister were born.

He was the old Colas then. A brilliant man, charming, seductive." He nodded in emphasis, "Yes, Colas was seductive. He was dangerous. You'd never forget the old Colas, believe me. But the new Colas, the blind Colas—he's a man of a different stamp, isn't he?"

"Father," Leonora interrupted. She laid her hand on the back of her father's wrist. He turned dark eyes on her. His face was thin and expressionless. He nodded, indicating that he would attend to her words.

Leonora repeated, "Father. Can you forgive me? This whole scheme was aimed at you. André and Kassia and I—"

"I know what your scheme was about," he cut her off. "There is nothing to forgive, daughter. Nothing to forgive you for. You were as much a dupe as I. You were lonely. You never got over the death of your sister, did you? Nor did I." His eyes misted.

"You're right. And—I suppose Kassia was like a new sister to me. So beautiful, so certain. I thought, why can't I be like her? And when she introduced me to André, I'm afraid I—"

"I understand," he put in. "And now André is dead, so that's an end to that." He held her hand in both of his.

"Tim."

Edmond shifted his eyes from his daughter's face to that of Kassia Paine.

"Perhaps—perhaps you might forgive me also," she managed.

"That is another matter," he said.

"I wouldn't blame you if you refused." She had picked up a small butter cookie and held it over her cup. Her hand trembled slightly and the cookie fell from her fingers and splashed into the hot, black coffee. A drop splashed onto her bare arm and she flinched; another stained her dress.

"It's just—" She paused and gazed at her hands. "Can you understand the spell that André Pavan could cast on women? I think it must have been supernatural."

"Probably not." Timothy Edmond rose from his seat, carried Kassia's coffee cup to the fireplace and threw its contents on the fire. There was a momentary hiss, then everything was as it had been. He returned to the women, refilled Kassia's cup and set it on the low table before her.

"I've seen men like that before, Kassia. There was a touch of André in Colas when I first knew him. Unlikely though that may seem. His type tend to prey on mousy little women. Shy, middle-aged spinsters with small inheritances. André—should I say, an André—will pay court to such a woman, convince her that he holds the key to her happiness. All her dreams of love, dreams that were fading with each turn of the calendar page, come back to vivid life. Sometimes he'll bed such a woman—forgive my indelicacy, Leonora dear—and sometimes not. But sooner or later he's gone, and so is her money. Either spent on fine clothing, shiny cars and high living for him, or carried away in his pocket. One way or another, he leaves his victim embittered, impoverished, and alone."

"Yes," Kassia agreed. Her face brightened. She leaned toward him.

"No." He shook his head. "André was the type, that's for certain. But you weren't. You're still beautiful and vibrant. I know that too well, Kassia. Much too well. André was a vampire preying on lonely middle-aged spinsters. You're another vampire, only your prey is foolish old men like me. Tired old men who are flattered by the attention of vibrant young women. Especially a beautiful one like you. Only you and André had a different scheme from the usual one. Instead of sipping from the throat, you would tear out the jugular with your blackmail scheme. Do you still have my letters? My stupid, schoolboy-crush *lettres-passionés?*"

She seemed flustered. Leonora drew back, horrified. Did Kassia still harbor some scheme against Timothy?

"I—well, I'm not sure where they are. We've been through so much, Leonora and I, and with André dead—old Colas spirited us away, got us to the roadway and promised to delay the investigation until we were out of France—Timmy-bear, Timmy-dear, I—"

His hand stung her face like a spider's venom. He pulled it back and stared at it in horror, his face as white as death. "I'm—I'm sorry. I shouldn't have struck you." He breathed once, twice, deeply. He spoke again, this time angrily. "Never use those names to me. Never again! *Never!*"

She leaned toward him. The firelight spun vortices in the swirls of her chignon. Her face was upturned, beneath his face, one side of her mannequin-perfect features reddened by the force of his blow, or perhaps simply by the warm reflection from the hearth.

He drew away from her as if she were a poisonous adder. "Use the letters," he hissed. "Use them and destroy me if you will. It will be an act of sheer spite, Kassia, I promise you. You will not receive a shilling from me. If you have a shred of decency in you, you will destroy them instead. Don't return them to me, I don't want to see them again. Just—keep them or destroy them or put them in the morning newspaper. It doesn't matter to me. All I can lose now is my reputation and my wealth. I care for neither, any longer."

He rose to his feet and summoned the butler once more. He said, "Malachi, please assist Miss Paine in any possible way. Help her with her things, arrange an air ticket to her home, drive her to the airport. She is leaving at once."

Kassia's eyes widened for a moment, then narrowed. She rose and backed away from him. She turned to Leonora. "Are you coming with me, then?"

Leonora looked from Kassia to her father, then back to Kassia. Without taking her eyes from the woman's face, she reached for her father's hand and took it in her own. She said, "It must be time for the spring showings in New York, Kassia. If you hurry you will be able to find work."

RICHARD A. LUPOFF *is the author of dozens of novels and nearly one hundred short stories. His most recent book,* Before . . . 12:01 . . . and After, *is a collection of short stories covering more than forty years. The title story of the collection has been the basis of several motion pictures. Lupoff's most recent novels are* The Cover Girl Killer *and* The Silver Chariot Killer.

The Outer Limits, Volume One

U.S. $12.00
Canada $16.95
ISBN: 0-7615-0619-5

"Soldier" by Harlan Ellison
A soldier on the battlefield can be a denizen of the past, the present, or the future. But the harrowing questions he faces transcend time. "Soldier," on which the famous 1964 *Outer Limits* episode was based, is a classic of the military science fiction sub-genre.

"It Crawled out of the Woodwork" by Diane Duane
Thirsting for power, there are always those among us who seek the ultimate—control over life and death. When offered the possibility of limitless power, a scientist discovers the dangerous lure of exploration on the edge of the unknowable.

"If These Walls Could Talk" by Howard Hendrix
You know what happens when the door to a haunted house is opened—boards creak, mysterious voices moan, danger is close at hand. But every haunted house is different, and the old Abrams house is not exactly what you'd expect.

"The Sixth Finger" by John M. Ford
A disturbing and memorable thought-experiment about an ordinary Welsh miner who is suddenly advanced through thousands of years of evolution.

The Outer Limits, Volume Two

U.S. $12.00
Canada $16.95
ISBN: 0-7615-0620-9

"The Choice" by Diane Duane
Aggie is a child with extraordinary powers — and no idea of how to control them. An organization of women with similar powers exists only to kidnap such girls and "save" them from the government's "experiments." Who will win the struggle for Aggie's life?

"Arena" by Fredric Brown
This intriguing account of controlled combat pits the heroes of two races in a struggle for the survival of their species. *Outer Limits* fans will recognize the roots of the 1960s episode "Fun and Games."

"The Message" by Richard A. Lupoff
When a deaf woman starts to hear for the first time, it should be good news. But what if all she can hear are incomprehensible "messages" from outer space, and the only person who believes her is a janitor with a record of mental illness?

"A Feasibility Study" by Michael Marano
When a government or a large corporation wants to try something new, it begins with a feasibility study. What if aliens are taking the same tack with their study to see if the human race is worth abducting?

The Trekker's Guide to The Next Generation® Complete, Unauthorized, and Uncensored

by Hal Schuster

U.S. $14.99
Canada $19.95
ISBN: 0-7615-0573-3

The Trekker's Guide to The Next Generation reveals what went into—and what was left out of—the seven television seasons and two feature films about the crew of the second starship Enterprise. Hal Schuster, a long-time, prominent chronicler of the Star Trek phenomenon, details just how the show was created and how it changed following the death of originator Gene Roddenberry.

Using information culled from interviews, the show's own bible, and other sources, *The Trekker's Guide to The Next Generation* takes you inside the popular show. Read character profiles and biographies of the actors who brought them to life. Get plot summaries for each of the 177 episodes and an insider's look at guest stars, innovations, and bloopers.

Totally unauthorized and uncensored, *The Trekker's Guide to The Next Generation* tells you what the producers at Paramount Pictures don't want you to know!

The Trekker's Guide to Voyager®
Complete, Unauthorized, and Uncensored

by Hal Schuster

U.S. $14.99
Canada $19.95
ISBN: 0-7615-0572-5

In *The Trekker's Guide to Voyager*, you'll learn what goes on both behind and in front of the camera in the words of the people closest to the events. Nowhere else will you find detailed biographies of the actors and production crew, complete character profiles, and in-depth specifications on every alien in the Delta Quadrant. Learn exactly why Genevieve Bujold quit the role of Captain Janeway just two days after she began work on the show. Discover why *Voyager* is the fourth series (including *Generations*) in which Tim Russ appears. And have you ever wondered just how far away the Delta Quadrant is? It's all here—and nowhere else.

Plus, *The Trekker's Guide to Voyager* features a special guide to the first two seasons of the show, along with a discussion of the oversights, inaccuracies, and outright blunders that mysteriously appear from time to time.

Completely uncensored, utterly fascinating, and intricately detailed, this book is the ultimate guide to *Star Trek: Voyager*.

Roger Zelazny and Jane Lindskold's
CHRONOMASTER

A Novel by Jane Lindskold

U.S. $5.99
Canada $6.99
ISBN: 0-7615-0422-2

The laws of physics have been repealed in the countless custom-made "pocket universes" of a strange new cosmos. Reality is variable and bottled time is as essential as oxygen.

But a mysterious stasis enshrouds two of these universes, threatening to spread to others. Inside, time has stopped. Who, or what, could be altering the pocket dimensions? And why?

Only Rene Korda, the retired planet sculptor and terraformer, understands artificial universes well enough to untangle the mystery. To find answers, Korda and his ship's meddlesome computer, Jester, embark on a journey that hurls them headlong into bizarre and dangerous dimensions unlike anything known before.

X-COM: UFO Defense

A Novel by Diane Duane

U.S. $5.99
Canada $6.99
ISBN: 0-7615-0235-1

Alien forces will enslave humanity unless X-COM can stop them. Commander Jonelle Barrett is determined to win. Having moved from Morocco to a new base in Switzerland, she is strategically well-prepared to build a fortified base and defend Europe from the marauding aliens who harvest humans as lab animals and for breeding stock . . . for their dinner tables.

Barrett soon finds that her new territory is already riddled with alien invaders. Her handpicked garrison is all she has — until she learns that one of her most trusted people may be a traitor. Her task is twofold: to keep the aliens at bay and to keep her own sanity in the face of despair. She doesn't know which will prove to be more difficult.

To Order Books

Please send me the following items:

Quantity	Title	Unit Price	Total
_____	_____	$ _____	$ _____
_____	_____	$ _____	$ _____
_____	_____	$ _____	$ _____
_____	_____	$ _____	$ _____
_____	_____	$ _____	$ _____

Shipping and Handling depend on Subtotal.

Subtotal	Shipping/Handling
$0.00–$14.99	$3.00
$15.00–$29.99	$4.00
$30.00–$49.99	$6.00
$50.00–$99.99	$10.00
$100.00–$199.99	$13.50
$200.00+	Call for Quote

Foreign and all Priority Request orders:
Call Order Entry department
for price quote at 916/632-4400

This chart represents the total retail price of books only
(before applicable discounts are taken).

Subtotal $ _____
Deduct 10% when ordering 3-5 books $ _____
7.25% Sales Tax (CA only) $ _____
8.25% Sales Tax (TN only) $ _____
5.0% Sales Tax (MD and IN only) $ _____
Shipping and Handling* $ _____
Total Order $ _____

By Telephone: With MC or Visa, call 800-632-8676 or 916-632-4400. Mon–Fri, 8:30–4:30

WWW: http://www.primapublishing.com

By Internet E-mail: sales@primapub.com

By Mail: Just fill out the information below and send with your remittance to:

**Prima Publishing
P.O. Box 1260BK
Rocklin, CA 95677**

My name is _____

I live at _____

City _____ State _____ ZIP _____

MC/Visa# _____ Exp. _____

Check/money order enclosed for $ _____ Payable to Prima Publishing

Daytime telephone _____

Signature _____